Charles Baxter

Harmony of the World

Charles Baxter is the author of two novels, *First Light* and *Shadow Play*, and three other collections of stories, *Through the Safety Net*, *A Relative Stranger*, and, most recently, a collection called *Believers*. He lives in Ann Arbor and teaches at the University of Michigan.

Also by Charles Baxter

Harmony of the World

Harmony

of the

World

Stories by

Charles Baxter

Vintage Contemporaries
Vintage Books
A Division of Random House, Inc.
New York

First Vintage Contemporaries Edition, March 1997

Some of the stories in this collection originally appeared in the following magazines:
The Antioch Review: "Xavier Speaking"
The Atlantic Monthly: "Horace and Margaret's Fifty-second"
Barney: "The Cliff"
Epoch: "The Model"
Michigan Quarterly Review: "Harmony of the World"
New England Review: "Gershwin's Second Prelude"
TriQuarterly: "Weights"
"Harmony of the World" appeared in *The Pushcart Prize VII* and *The Best American Short Stories 1982*.

The author wishes to acknowledge a grant from the National Endowment for the Arts, which gave time to complete this book.

Library of Congress Cataloging-in-Publication Data
Baxter, Charles, 1947–
Harmony of the world : stories / by Charles Baxter.—1st Vintage contemporaries ed.
p. cm.—(Vintage contemporaries)
Contents: Gershwin's Second prelude—Xavier speaking—The model—Horace and Margaret's fifty-second—The cliff—A short course in Nietzschean ethics—The would-be father—Weights—Harmony of the world—The crank.
ISBN 0-679-77651-6
I. Title.
PS3552.A854H3   1997
813'.54—dc20   96-31639
CIP

Random House Web address: http://www.randomhouse.com/

Printed in the United States of America
10 9 8 7 6 5 4 3 2 1

For Martha

Contents

Gershwin's Second Prelude

While Kate practiced the piano in the tiny third-floor apartment, Wiley cooked dinner, jogging in place in front of the stove. His feet made the pans clatter, and, after twenty minutes of exercise, he began to hyperventilate. He stopped, took his pulse, then continued, jogging to the spice rack, to the refrigerator's butter shelf, then back to the stove. The air smelled of cumin, chicken stock, and tomatoes—something Mexican. The noise was terrible. He knocked over a spatula. A bottle of soda fell into the catfood dish. Worse yet, he hummed tunes from his high school prom days, melodies like "Call Me Mister Blue" and "Dream Lover," in a nasal, plaintive whine. The noise diverted Kate's attention and broke her Schubert sonatas into small pieces of musical trash.

That day at lunch, Kate's friend Sarah had told her to put an end to her passivity in the face of this uproar. "Tell him to shut up," she said. "Wiley's a narcissist. You have to tell him everything twice. I introduced you to him, so I know."

Kate nodded.

Sarah bit into a carrot and continued. "It was probably a mistake. Wiley has sinister friends. If I were you, I'd get rid of him fast, before those creeps show up in their Halloween masks. Have you ever watched him comb his hair? Of course you have. He stands for half an hour in front of the mirror. I've seen him put aftershave *into* his hair, right down at the scalp. Nobody does that. I'm sorry, but he's disgusting. He'll never love you."

"I know," Kate said. She couldn't afford to eat out and was taking her omelette in tiny bites.

"He's just living in your apartment because you gave him a bed to flop in." Sarah stopped for a minute, took a long sip of water, and then touched her eyelid with her little

finger. "I'm sorry to be crude, but that's how it is. I shouldn't
have introduced you two. I feel terrible about it. Will you
forgive me?"
Kate nodded. "Sure. Anyway, I don't mind Wiley. You
know why? He makes me laugh."
"Makes you laugh? Watch 'The Flintstones' if you want
to laugh. But don't keep that loser around."
"He's a good cook. He makes our meals."
"He's a chef, for heaven's sake. That's his *job*. That's why
he's a good cook." She stopped. "You love him, don't you?"
Kate shrugged. "I know he's a loser, but losers make me
laugh. Things don't matter to them anymore, and they treat
life like a joke." She put her fork down. "Winners make
ugly lovers," she said with finality. "I don't want that."

"No more Schubert," said Madame Gutowski in her studio, one flight up from Buster's Subs 'n' Suds. Madame
Gutowski was an old woman, and her voice came out in a
breathy rattle. In her studio the paint was flaking off the
ceiling; mice, or worse, were inside the walls. Kate had
finished the second movement of the Schubert B-flat so-
nata while the old woman had scowled and tapped her
fingers on the edge of the chair. "No more Schubert," she
repeated irritably. "You play like an American. You speed
up the tempo to make a climax. This is Schubert, not Las
Vegas. Too much, too much effort to please the customers.
The score does not say to accelerate. You make it too pathetic. Also you make it silly. Has been played like this."
Madame rolled her hand into a tight fist, shaking it in Kate's
face. "Should be played like this." She relaxed her hand
and waved goodbye. "Schubert stands at the door, lends
handkerchief, gives good wishes, says, 'Farewell, farewell.' But he knows the sky is getting dark. Always he knows
this. That is Schubert." She shook her head. "You seem
unable to learn the style."
"Maybe I could learn some new Chopin," Kate suggested. "Chopin instead of Schubert. The impromptus or
the—"
"—Chopin?" Madame whispered, before making a
clucking sound. "No no no no no no. He is not ready for

you. He waits up ahead, is standing inside summer house, head down, listening to sky and grass, thinking about love and anger." She continued to whisper. "I consider Chopin all the time. He is very close to me. *He talks*." Madame leaned back and stared at Kate, pretending surprise at her own revelation. She returned to her normal voice. "You are too young for him. You have some growing to do. Maturing. He is not for you. Not while you are playing this way, in this girlish American style."

"I'm not a girl," Kate sighed. "But you could teach me to play Chopin. Your style."

"No. You must learn how to be calm as you sit at piano. Chopin will wait for you. *I* will wait for you. I will introduce you to him. But not yet! He likes quickness but not quite so much push."

Kate leaned back and looked out of the window at the grime-streaked traffic. It, too, had a great deal of push. Then, inside, her gaze fell first on Madame's cane leaning against the overstuffed chair, then on the lady's bony fingers. Long-term arthritis made the knuckles look like popcorn. "What do you suggest?" she asked. "Beethoven? Beethoven has a lot of push."

"No," Madame said. "Gershwin."

"Gershwin?" Kate frowned. "That's trash."

"No. Is *not* trash. Get 'Three Preludes,' learn number two. It is a good piece for Americans. Is hard, requires wizard, but teaches tenderness from first bar to end. You Americans have such trouble learning tenderness, I don't understand. Learn to relax into calm. We start next week." Madame glared angrily at her watch.

Kate stood up and bowed, as instinctively she always had. "Thank you, Madame," she said.

The old woman nodded without looking at Kate. "Gershwin, a nice boy. You two will adore each other."

Kate left, annoyed as usual that Madame never looked her in the eye.

At the institute, Kate sat in front of her telephone, collecting data, or "social research" as it was called. Each day's work kit included a list of numbers to dial, chosen with

guaranteed randomness by a computer, and a small pile of
questionnaires. An electric clock the size of a large pizza
hummed on the wall above her. The clock obsessed her in
an unhealthy way. She considered it her enemy. In a nearby
glassed-in office, her supervisor monitored all the calls to
make sure that the interviews were both discreet and suc-
cessful. The other women at the institute were all younger
than Kate and had taken the job interviewing people they
didn't know as a diversion until the job they really wanted
came along. For some reason, the institute didn't like to
hire men; they had tried it, but the men hadn't stayed for
more than three days or so. Something about the job was
intolerable to people with ambitions. The average employee stayed around for about three months. Kate had set
a record at the institute: she had been there for four years.

"You know," Wiley said, picking his teeth with a pocket-
knife after dinner, "I once worked as a circus clown. I may
again."

"What?"

"A circus clown. You didn't know that, did you?"

"No," Kate said. "There's a lot I don't know about you."

"You said the truth," Wiley agreed. "But the fact is, I always liked to hang around with those show people, you
know, the carnival types. I'll tell you how I got to be a clown.
It was in my Joe College days, when I was so straight that
I thought people were real. It was one of those junior-year-
abroad deals, and I was in Amsterdam. I was supposed to
be working in a Dutch mental hospital, and I was, with
part of my brain, but with the other part I'd gotten mixed
up with some lowdown importer-exporters." He stopped,
leaned his head back, and laughed. "I guess I wasn't so
straight. Anyway, I was headed downtown one day for a
meeting with a guy I didn't want to see, and I passed by a
large brown door with a sign next to it. The sign said that
the place was the one and only School for Fools."

"School for Fools?"

"Yup. A clown college. Biggest one in the world. They
teach makeup, pratfalls, balancing, and all sorts of routines. I tried it out for a while. When I got back to the states,

I worked as a clown for a couple of weeks during the summer on a state-fair midway. In Minnesota." He nodded. "The
land of ten thousand lakes." He nodded again. "I never got
my college diploma. But I learned about crowds."

"What's it like, being a clown?"

"Well, working as a salad chef is easier. They pay you
more. By the way, I need to borrow some money from you.
I almost forgot. But, as I was saying, a circus clown needs
timing, which is essentially the hard part. He's usually
taught first how to tumble, how to take falls, then how to
do pratfalls and stand on his hands. Like I say, though, it's
mostly timing."

"You never told me this."

"We're strangers, Kate."

"I know, but it seems so interesting." She smiled. "Can
you still do a pratfall? Is it painful?"

Wiley got up from the dinnertable. "Of course it's not
painful. You just have to know how to do it." As he stood,
he let his body go loose in an effort to relax. He lit a cigarette and said, "All right. Suppose you're in the audience.
Now imagine I've just been kicked real hard from behind."

Kate nodded, feeling shy.

"Okay," Wiley said. "Watch."

All at once his mouth opened in an expression of clown-
shock, his eyebrows flew up, and his legs shot out in front
of him, his body hanging there momentarily as if held by
invisible wires before it dropped to the floor, making the
dinner dishes rattle.

"Good God, Wiley," Kate said, laughing. "Jesus. You *are*
a clown. That's terrific. Can you walk on your hands?"

"Not only can I walk on my hands," Wiley said, "but I
can walk on my hands and play your piano with my feet.
Are you going to lend me fifty bucks or not?"

"Of course, of course."

Wiley jumped, stood on his hands, his change falling out
of his pockets, and walked on his hands out of the dining
room, into the living room, where he lowered his feet to
hit the piano keys. He stood up and walked back to the
table.

"See?" he asked. "A real clown. Kate, I need that money tonight, before I go off to work."

In the bedroom, Kate searched through her dresser drawer where she thought she had stashed seventy dollars. She could only find forty of it, but she picked it up and clenched it in her right hand.

"Here," she said. "It's all I've got left."

"Forty?" He sighed. "Oh, all right." He made a face. "I've got to go to work." He squatted down, put his hands under her arms to lift her up, and, when she was standing, he put his arms around her and held her for a long time, kissing her mouth and her forehead. When he was finished, Kate felt her heart's rhythms beginning to pick up, along with her breath rate. She leaned hard against him.

"Oh don't leave yet," she said, trying to whisper. "Stay for a few minutes."

"Later, Kate," he said. "Good love takes time."

"I can't sit around waiting for you," she said as he drew away. "I can't."

"You will."

She understood that, despite his passionate embrace and kiss, he wasn't physically aroused at all. His responses were unpredictable: he could stay physically indifferent to her as he managed, simultaneously, to lead her into the greatest sexual feelings she had ever experienced. She sometimes felt as if he treated her body as if he were a scientist, experimenting to see what he could do to it.

After he left, Kate sat at the dinnertable for an hour, imagining that Wiley had walked down to the drugstore at the corner to buy some antihistamine. "I've lived with different guys," she said aloud to herself, "but never with a circus clown." She was collecting the dirty dishes and putting them to soak in the kitchen sink when the phone rang.

"Hi, Kate," Wiley said. "It's me. I'm under arrest."

"Wiley, what happened?"

"They said I was shoplifting."

Gershwin's second prelude is marked "Andante con moto e poco rubato," and as soon as she tried to play it, later that week, Kate discovered that she would have to tinker with the rhythms in order to project the feeling Madame would expect. Her own feelings of nervousness about Wiley she kept out of the music. The prelude sounded like the blues—white urban blues—and as she worked through the cross-over fingerings, she imagined a fitting scene for the melody: a well-tailored man standing on a penthouse balcony gazes over a city just after sunset. His building's empty elevators rise and descend automatically throughout the early evening. He thinks of a joke that fails to amuse him. Lights in the other buildings come on. F. Scott Fitzgerald appears, Zelda drunk on his arm.

Wiley was out on bail. That afternoon, Kate had discovered a hypodermic needle in the medicine cabinet, hidden behind Wiley's electric shaver.

"Posture!" Madame Gutowski snapped, knocking once on the side of the piano bench with her cane. "Remember always posture! Be relaxed but alert. You sit like killer in electric chair. Stiff, guilty of crimes. Remember to let hands rest on keys, relaxed but alert. And *lean forward!* Music leans forward."

Kate looked down at her hands, trying to make them more alert than they were. They felt like sea slugs, unable to achieve anything like consciousness. Perhaps they knew, in their dumb animal way, that Madame wouldn't care for what they were about to do.

"Play," Madame commanded. "Demonstrate Gershwin."

The left hand stretched out and began. Together it and the right hand did what they could, while Kate tried to imagine that lonely soul in the penthouse overlooking the city park, but, as she played, she felt herself losing that image as another one took its place: a semitrailer truck unloading a ton of damp saltines.

"Concentrate," Madame whispered. "Do not fight with your mind."

Then she pictured Wiley shooting up a small, discreet quantity of junk before he walked—no, *sailed*—off to his evening chores as a salad chef.

"Play notes on page," Madame instructed. "Do not swing the rhythm. Do not try to jazz it."

Kate worked her way to the last chord and waited, hands in lap, for Madame to speak. From downstairs she heard the cook in Buster's Subs 'n' Suds calling an order of two chili dogs to the kitchen. Madame stared at her, then said, "You have not met Gershwin yet. He is still inside the piano trying to get out. Play the piece again for me. Remember that the goal of prelude is not to arrive at doublebar line, like a train pulling into a depot. The goal is to express tenderness, as landscape flows past."

Kate repeated the piece as Madame's jaw worked with what Kate thought might be senile anger.

Kate had been on the phone to Sarah again.

"You didn't tell me that Wiley's a junky," she said.

"Oh Jesus. Is he? I didn't know that. Christ. But you can't blame me, Kate. I only lived with him for two weeks."

"He's been arrested for shoplifting," Kate announced, her voice creeping toward tonelessness. "Why did you introduce us?" She stopped. "Why did you bring him over here?"

"Well, he *is* so funny. At first. You know Wiley. I wanted to get him off my back, I guess. Sorry, Kate. Really, you've got to dump him."

"How?"

"Introduce him to somebody else."

Wiley's ideas about music were superficial and narrative: he enjoyed putting Kate's recording of Mahler's second symphony on the phonograph and explaining what the music meant, minute by minute. "Here," Wiley droned, "Mahler is trying to put on his overshoes. But they won't fit. Mahler goes into the kitchen and has a big argument with Mrs. Mahler." (Here the orchestra played fortissimo.) "But Mrs. Mahler resists! She tells Gustav that overshoes aren't her department! *'Liebchen,'* she says, 'leave me alone with my strudel.' Mahler exits to conduct the Vienna State Opera Orchestra in his French Shriners." (The music's level went down to mezzoforte.) "But on the way, Mahler falls into a mud puddle."

Despite herself, Kate was amused by this patter; she liked

to have music humiliated occasionally. Making music look
cheap was Wiley's line, and Kate enjoyed it.

"Wiley," Kate interrupted, "I found something a few days
ago that I wanted to ask you about."

"Yeah? What?"

"A hypodermic in the medicine chest."

Wiley nodded. "I know about it."

"What's it doing there?"

"It's mine."

"What are *you* doing with it?"

"Engine tune-ups."

"No, really." She had to shout to be heard above the music.

"What do you think it's for?" He smiled. "A diabetic condition?"

"You're not diabetic. Do you shoot up?"

He turned the music off. Then he nodded. "Sometimes,"
he said. "When I'm in the mood. You aren't going to be
American and get all hysterical about this, are you? Because there's nothing to be hysterical about. When they talk
about it on television, it's all lies. How do I know? I know
because I know."

"Why do you do it?"

"I like to feel like God," Wiley said. "I like to have the
sun explode and then spray over my face." He stood up
and walked over to her. "And I think you should try it. I
honestly honestly do. If anyone is ready for a little taste of
shit, Kate darling, that person is Kate."

"No."

Wiley sank to his knees and clasped his hands in her lap.
"I can turn your whole spine into a Christmas tree. Colored
lights, Kate, and blue and red ornaments hanging on your
heart. Listen to me. You could be a bright star. You could
make your brain into a success."

"Wiley, where do you get this stuff?"

"You don't want to know them." He shuddered. "The
pleasure gets to you by way of riffraff."

"I don't get it," Kate said. "You jog and you eat health
foods. But you shoot up this stuff? What's the connection?"

"The body," Wiley said without hesitation. "The body is
the theater, the scene. I like to experiment with it. Some-

times I get a little bored with the theater of life, so I do the
theater of death. The theater of death is pleasure. Still silent solitary pleasure. It's not like anything happens in pure
pleasure. Nothing does. It's the pleasure of death, you
understand?" He looked at his watch and stood up.
"Oooops. Time to go to work." He bent down to kiss her,
and she felt his tongue flick against her ear lobe. "Bye,
kitten."

Kate usually woke up when Wiley came in at two o'clock,
but when the door didn't open and Wiley failed to drop his
boots in the foyer, failed to go to the refrigerator for a beer,
and failed to turn on Dr. Tormento's All Night Terror Theater, she lay awake with the light burning. The digital clock
glowed. She watched the numbers attentively. Three o'clock
had no funny stories. Four o'clock, the worst hour in the
night, had character but no tenderness. Five o'clock was
the alarm going off for the sun; its light glowed like an infection in the east. At six all was not well. At seven she
knew Wiley was in trouble, and at eight he walked in, his
face bloody. He collected his clothes and records, would
not say anything, smiled at her, then left. Kate grabbed
onto his shirt as he walked down the stairs.
    "Oh no," he said. "No. I don't ever explain."
    Kate had turned thirty that month. With Wiley gone, she
thought of her past, of the music scholarships, the lost jobs,
the men, the empty bank accounts. She thought of her parents. They didn't like to call her because she just gave them
bad news. "Success is counted sweetest / By those who
ne'er succeed," wrote Emily Dickinson, poet of the dor-
mouse experience, and Kate's favorite writer. Kate's mind
was full of questions, but the mind refused to answer them.
She stared at Wiley's pencil life study of her, where her
body had been drawn with specific tenderness.

    "He left me," she told Sarah.
    "Good riddance."
    "You don't understand. I'm alone."
    "So?"
    "I don't like it."

"Learn to live with it. He was a creep."

"That's easy for you to say. You're married. I never had sex the way I had it with him. He broke through to something in me."

"I'm not married, I'm separated. There's a difference. Why'd he leave?"

"I asked him about the hypodermic. He left the next day."

"You're better off than you were before."

"And you have children, too. So don't tell me how wonderful it is being alone. You haven't been alone for seven years. You don't know anything about it."

"Kate, I *do* understand. I am lonely sometimes."

"Also," Kate continued, "you've never failed at having a career. You have kids, a husband who may come back to you, and for two weeks you had Wiley. He wasn't good enough for you. He was just a piece of male trash, a piece of garbage you threw out. Okay, he wasn't good enough for you, but he looked all right to me. You've never lost out on anything, Sarah, so don't go sermonizing to me." She swallowed. "Because you don't know what you're talking about."

The bus having arrived fifteen minutes too early in front of Madame's studio, Kate went into Buster's Subs 'n' Suds and ordered a torpedo sandwich and a glass of red wine. It was her sixth glass of wine since noon: she had left work, claiming illness, and had walked to a cafe to read Doris Lessing and to drink wine. She had succeeded at both. Now, realizing she was drunk, she studied the other diners until they noticed her; then she turned away. From upstairs, filtered through the grease-flecked ceiling, came music from Madame's baby grand Mason and Hamlin: chords and passages with bizarre contours, the luminously structural madness of Scriabin. Kate thought that the sandwich would sober her up, but when two identical waitresses came toward her, carrying the check, she knew it hadn't.

At exactly four o'clock she walked upstairs, tripping on one step, and knocked. Madame shouted, "Come in!" and Kate entered. Madame was seated at the piano, bent over the keyboard as if weeping, her long thin fingers rushing

up and down in a grotesque way. Kate shivered. Madame
had known Enesco and Bartók. She had once played for
Ravel. Ravel hadn't just applauded; Ravel had stood up.
Arthritis had put an end to Madame's career in the 1940s.
Without knowing what Madame was playing, Kate knew
it wasn't being played correctly, that it was being damaged,
that Ravel would no longer applaud.

Madame stopped, turned, and looked at Kate. She
pointed one bent finger at Kate's mouth. "Food. Please wipe
it off." Kate took a tissue from her purse and licked it before
cleaning the mustard stains on her chin. The wine made
her feel both drunk and sleepy. She hardly knew where
she was. She rubbed and rubbed at her chin until the skin
felt raw.

Madame lifted herself off the piano bench with her cane,
half-sat, half-fell into her usual chair, and barked at Kate.
"Sit. Play Gershwin, correctly. It is a new day today, I know
it. Concentrate on tenderness this time."

Though she had double vision, Kate had been practicing
the piece regularly, and at first the wine gave her courage.
She was halfway through when Madame sat up. "No!" she
said. "It is *worse* than before! Incredibly! Is much worse!
You are not reading notes on page. *Poco* rubato, little one,
not *molto*! Pedal use is very poor: all clear notes turning
indistinct. Too much slurring. Whining and pausing and
stopping for breath. Why do you insist on playing this way?
This style of self-pity?"

Kate stopped. Her hands went limp. She absent-mindedly
took out a cigarette, lit it, inhaled, and with it between her
fingers she started the piece again. Before she remembered
that she was at her weekly piano lesson, and not at home,
Madame exploded. "What is that?"

"Oh shit," Kate said, instantly blushing. She tried to stub
the cigarette out on the wood floor near the pedals. The
cigarette stuck to her sandal and she had to pick it off with
her fingers before throwing it out of the window. "Madame," she said. "I'm sorry. I forgot you were there. I've
been smoking lately."

"I smell wine also," the old woman said, her teeth chat-
tering.

"Yes. I'm drunk." Coming back from the window, Kate sat on the bench and looked Madame in the eye. "You know, Madame," she said in an undertone, "I'm a nitwit."

"A what?"

"A nitwit." She pointed at her head. "Nothing but cotton up here. I have a silly job. I fall in love with ridiculous men. I fill myself up with nicotine and alcohol. No talent. I'm not a serious woman."

Madame's eyes stared at her, clear and hawklike. "What? What is this nicotine? You mean morphia?"

"No, that's Wiley. Wiley does that. Me, I just smoke cigarettes. Oh, and the wine."

"Who is Wiley?"

"This man. He just left me."

"You have tried morphia also?"

"No. Never."

There was a long pause. Then Madame leaned back. "Now listen. You children think you are so new with your misery, with your morphia. Pain always seems new when you have it. And I admit: grief gets in the way of playing piano. It mixes you up. But listen." She tilted her head back and closed her eyes. "Imagine Paris in 1928. I was studying and playing. *Very* young. You have heard the names of people I knew. I will not mention them. Ravel, many others. For a time, possibility was everywhere. We had been through the war and that was that."

"So much talent around," Kate said.

Madame waved her hand like a broken flag. "Yes, yes. But they were busy all day, working. You do not see artists in bars drinking wine. They are busy in their rooms, they have *schedules!*" Madame scowled for a moment. "But do not interrupt me. As I said, there was much happiness then, with the war gone away and hundreds of new ideas coming into practice. I was then your age, maybe younger. Like you, very talented. A small bit more talented, but the difference is not important. Basically I sat at piano five, six hours a day.

"So, a beautiful place. Everyone said so. 'Aren't you lucky to be here, Clara?' they said to me. I always said, 'Yes.' And I had a friend." Madame closed her eyes and nodded. "A

beautiful young man, a painter: oils, watercolors, ex-cubist.
He was given attention in galleries and salons. The critics
noticed him. For one year we had each night a rendezvous
before dinner, when the light was useless for painting and
piano practice time was over. We took walks in the Bois.
We made dinner for friends. Attended concerts and open-
ings. We talked often, often, about future. Then, the end."
Madame stopped and waited. "No future after all."

"Why?"

Madame nodded, pleased that Kate was listening. "I will
tell you. Remember what you have read about Paris. Now
the books say there was only happiness and creative fire. I
arrived, a little girl from Poland. I was introduced to groups.
Then, a girl, I discover what everyone has always known.
Joy is infected. Joy for too long is infection. Cannot last.
My painter disappears, then turns up to see me with his
face all cloudy. I ask him why, and he says, 'Opium.' Well.
Some it doesn't hurt. But others, the weak little happy ones
get it but do not get over it. They fall into it like falling into
a lake of diamonds. They don't come up. More joy. *Too much
joy!* You have heard maybe of Cocteau?"

Kate nodded.

"Talented, but oh, he was silly. He had a weakness for
happiness, that one. Clutched at it all the time. He thought
boredom was not real, Cocteau. A big mistake. So my
painter, who like Cocteau is finding this opium, he tries to
stop but does *not* stop. He loses his vision for painting. His
ideas go away. What does he spend his day thinking about?
I don't know. He won't tell me. He says there are no more
pictures. He says: 'Color is too much work.' Too much work!
To me, he looks more and more like a man turning around,
on his way back to his mother. One afternoon, we drink
champagne together. We walk together by Seine to Notre
Dame. He says maybe he will convert, be a Catholic as I
am, safe in God's arms. Maybe he will solve problems of
soul. We walk upstairs to the top of the cathedral, to see
Paris to the west. He cries with happiness, with arrange-
ment of cloud light. Then he lifts himself up, says, '*Au fu-
tur*,' and puts his foot on top of a gargoyle face. He takes a

leap, aaiiee, into space. He broke like an egg below. He lived for three hours, speaking to ghosts."

"I'm sorry."

"Do *not* be sorry. Congratulate me for living in Paris for ten more years, alone. Congratulate me for coming here, for losing career, for opening a studio over a restaurant. Congratulate me for teaching slow clucks and dumb bunnies. Congratulate me for avoiding infection, for having not too much happiness."

"Congratulations," Kate said.

"Boredom has its own tenderness, its own mercy," Madame said softly. "Now tell me. Will you not celebrate with wine constantly, from now on? Will you not try to be happy, always?"

"I promise. Cross my heart."

"Then give me my cane."

Kate reached over to where the cane leaned against the Mason and Hamlin's shiny black wood and gave it to Madame. The old woman put both hands over it and lifted herself up. Standing, her shoulders bent, she said, "Already you are learning. You will become a hero. You will learn to face losses of giant size. That requires ceremony. It requires champagne. We will drink."

"Do you have champagne here?" Kate asked. The studio was bare except for the piano and Madame's chair.

"Of course not. It will have to be imagined. Raise glass."

"What about my piece? What about Gershwin?"

"Poor boy. He died of a brain tumor when young. Do as I say!"

Kate watched the old woman prop herself on her cane, as her right hand lifted into the air, the thumb and forefingers holding an invisible glass. If there had been a glass, a real one, it would have been shaking, because the old woman trembled with anger and passion, and the champagne would have spilled out over Madame's thin, veiled wrist.

"Raise glass!" Madame shouted. "Stand!"

Kate stood and after a moment hoisted her right hand, thumb and forefinger in a circle broken by a gap for the invisible stem, until the glass that was not there had reached the level of her shoulder. The old woman, seeing that she had done so, suddenly shot at her an utterly fierce and impersonal smile.

"Drink!" she commanded. Kate watched her, then drank.

Xavier Speaking

Not very long ago, Doubleday published a book by Sara Davidson called *Loose Change: Three Women of the Sixties*. It was heavily advertised and subsequently made into a television movie, which Davidson disowned. The book's essays concern three roommates at Berkeley and what happens to them during a period of cultural shift. Their cases are somewhat atypical, however: all three women are articulate, attractive, and intelligent. Fate sends them to medical school, or the publishing world, or small tasteful galleries on the upper East Side. It is a peculiarly American story, with more than a small echo of Horatio Alger.

A few weeks after the book came out, I received a letter from Arthur, a friend from college who has time-capsuled himself in rural Wisconsin, some miles north of Rhinelander. Where Arthur lives, the sixties try to survive, and from time to time I find these letters—recipes, lectures, poems, and manifestoes (like Ezra Pound's correspondence)— waiting for me in the mailbox. Arthur wanted to know about Davidson's book. "You buy those things," he wrote, referring to mass-market hardbacks, "and I want to know what's in this one." So I bought *Loose Change*, read it, and sent it on to him. He was enraged. "This book is about nothing I know," he wrote me in a furious review-letter. "It is about one thing: *looking for the right doctor*" (his emphasis). I should add that Arthur and I both turned thirty that year, and I understand how easy it is to turn frosty with anger when someone explains our youth to us. But Arthur's letter went on and on, a traitor to that equanimity he had worked so hard to preserve. At some point, looking at the letter's ink stains next to underlinings and erasures, I realized that Arthur felt *his* life was exemplary; *he* should be in Davidson's book. Other lives, for him, were not exemplary. To him, my life is an example of nothing in particular; it is just a life. Which is why he sends me these pedantic letters: he wants me to be somebody. Out there, on his farm in Wisconsin, he is sure of his selfhood. I think I know how he achieved this sense of identity, and I think I also know how I turned my back on it.

Arthur's major changed six times in his freshman year, 1965. Up until then, he had loved experiments, their noise and complexity. So he began with physics, moved to chemistry, switched from that to biology, made a leap across to psychology until he grew weary of rat behavior; then he wandered into political science and finally landed in history, with a minor in astronomy ("I'm interested in constellations"). In those days history majors were still getting jobs, but his commitment to the humanities was slow. He liked the "hard" disciplines, the masculine reach of the calculus. What sent him out of the sciences, however, was not a distaste for the subject matter but a distaste for the experiments he had once loved. "I'm getting tired of the data heap," he told me.

In physics, he handled radioactive materials; in chemistry, he created explosives; in biology, he pithed and dissected toads ("they make these horrible croaking sounds when they croak"); in psychology he ran rats across electrified grids; in political science, he learned game theory and played war games on a map with bloody red splotches.

For the first few months I knew him, he had a plain, almost insipid Midwestern face, the kind of Scandinavian blank slate that women sometimes find attractive. But as these experiments went on, and the pile of dead toads and shocked rats grew, his face began to change: in the dialectical heat of his anger, some presence established itself behind his pale blue eyes until even he knew that he had become somebody, a man who refused to do certain things. His face hollowed, and a mustache sprouted on it. I noticed that when he said almost anything to women, they either laughed or looked very serious.

His other life, the social one, was busy—busier than mine or anyone else's I knew. His anger, being itself electrical, magnetized others, and with his faint touch of decadence he attracted a long line of young women who traipsed through his room. Here, as in the switch of majors, Arthur began with experiments but stopped as soon as he discovered that they could produce results. He felt that there were methods, not in themselves very complex, that could be used to drive women crazy. He told me how he had provoked certain mild sexual frenzies, using the tone not of a libertine but of a sorcerer's apprentice. When I listened to the stories of his sexual adventures, I felt as though I were being taken to a distant country whose customs could never be transposed to this one. "The real question," he said, "is whether you *want* everything you can *have*. I don't." A year after he made this remark, he was married.

His wife, now his ex-wife, I will call Carrie, and since she stands as the unsignified signifier at the center of this tale, I won't characterize her very much. They met, not at a political rally, but at a midwinter college dance, called the Sno-Ball. They talked long enough to take an interest in each other, and for Arthur, who had a good memory for names, to get hers (his date was in the powder room at the time). Their reliance on small talk and smiles to get acquainted did not seem inappropriate in 1966.

Strips of white paper hung down from the ceiling; bits of white tissue in imitation of snow littered the floor. The picturebook couples two-stepped beneath posters of Vail and Aspen, skiers flying through the air in dynamic but frozen postures, like paratroopers. I helped decorate the room. I can remember lighting the student union's ballroom with soft blue fuzz spotlights: it made the flakes look "romantic" like early Technicolor snow. Undergraduate men still wore cologne, at least in Minnesota; I had a bottle of pungent green stuff I bought at Rexall for sixty-nine cents. It was the last time anybody could remember dressing up *in that way*, because the following year the omnipresence of lying made straight costumes suddenly sinister. Outside, a real blizzard started halfway through the evening.

When Arthur first slept with Carrie, he had to remove all the stuffed animals from her bed. Her boyfriend's picture looked at them from the desk, and Jesus looked at them from the wall. Because the noise of lovemaking upset her, she kept the radio tuned to a "beautiful music" station that played selections like Percy Faith's "Harbor Lights" repeatedly without pause, as if for a grocery store of nervous shoppers. Arthur told me later, "Her consciousness had a long way to rise."

Several months later the three of us were talking about Vietnam, the increasing troop levels, and strategies for evading the draft, when Arthur announced that *he*, for one, would not be concerned about the army, because he and Carrie were going to be married. Carrie smiled, and I managed with an insect voice to congratulate them. It struck me then that he found her structural innocence attractive.

An interlude: for them, marriage and politics arrived simultaneously. Arthur and Carrie read Fanon, Norman O. Brown, and Cleaver to each other, took classes on social thought together, picked up the Civil Rights movement (a bit too late—they folded from that participation), listened to music, smoked first dope, then hash, then, sitting on the bank of the Mississippi River on the St. Paul side, dropped LSD. Arthur saw his sister, two years dead, waving to him from a barge. In every sense they became representative of, as my family would say, "a certain class of people." Their clothes changed, looking more homemade every day; then their language changed. Carrie inherited some money, and they had an all-night session on whether to keep it. They did. They marched, picketed, threw things. Then, abruptly, they bought a farm in Wisconsin. "Paradise is inside, is in the land," Arthur said, six months after having tear gas shot at him, after being arrested and locked up. "Good dirt is a drug," he'd say. "I'm gonna be listening for earth sounds." They moved.

The standard wisdom about ventures like theirs (samples in *Easy Rider* or *The Eden Express* or even *The Blithedale Romance*) is that farming is a complicated business, that you can't have crazies out there in the fields mooning over the seeds and expect the whole operation to thrive; prayer and faith cannot replace good old American know-how. And so forth. Apparently Arthur learned somewhere what is now published for general knowledge in places like the *Mother Earth News*, because although they were, in his words, "shockingly poor," they weren't hungry and they did have a little money. Crops were planted, cultivated; they came up and were harvested. A postcard: "We aren't dying out here. Living alive is a success."

Gardens and paradise. They wanted a baby. They tried with, as Arthur said, "the gloves off." Nothing. They both went to be checked, and Arthur discovered that he was sterile. To fill time, they bought a television set that, over the phone, they claimed they never watched. When Carrie came on the line, all she said was, "I've never had one and already I miss it." She laughed. I couldn't tell what she was talking about.

I had finished my first year in graduate school at Buffalo and was invited out to their farm in the summer of 1971. Driving there, I wondered what sort of place would be called "Rhinelander." Rhine land: Wagner country. But it was a modest landscape of pine woods, lakes, and very dark fields, almost inky black, evidently quite fertile. They greeted me in a haze of mosquitoes. I heard pigs grunting some distance away, and I smelled slops.

Two days later, noon: on an army blanket spread out under a boxelder tree, Arthur, Carrie, and I were eating lunch: cheese, nuts, tomatoes, leaf lettuce, and hardboiled eggs. Off in the distance, the chickens were milling around, and Arthur kept his eye on them to make sure they didn't wander onto the county road nearby. I felt sunburned; they were both heavily and unevenly tanned from outdoor work. Arthur wiped his forehead so the sweat wouldn't fall into his eyes. I had been weeding in the vegetables with him, and my hands tingled, felt raw and itchy. In the middle of Arthur's shirt a heart-shaped blot of sweat was slowly enlarging and reaching toward his shoulders, and, as it did, Carrie slapped her left foot, killing a mosquito.

"Good food," I said, pleased with my reawakened ability to taste.

"Thank you," Arthur said, suddenly smiling. "That's a

compliment we can accept. You think a lot about food out
here. You have to. That's probably where the whole Movement went."

"Where?"

"It ended up on the plates. Diets changed. The politics
evolved so that people couldn't eat the way they always
had. We couldn't get the government structures, but we
could get the supermarkets. Maybe not you, but at least
us. And you get the idea."

Carrie said, "Puritanism lives on in the way people eat.
Only someone who would want to punish his body would
eat the fast food they're selling now. How can you think
straight after a meal like that? It's violent food. Eating those
hamburgers is like being hit in the face. You get punchy
after a while. If we ate better, there wouldn't have been
Vietnam or Nixon."

I said nothing in response to this outrageousness, but I
did look more closely at Carrie. Dangling down from her
neck, I noticed, was a cross, large enough to suggest true
belief. Arthur saw me looking at it.

"Carrie has faith," he said simply.

"That's the revolution, too," she told me. "Christ is a man
but he is also food—it's all connected: what people put in
their mouths and their eyes comes out in the way they think.
Lately when I've been reading the Gospels I've discovered
how much they're about eating. Seeds, fish, loaves of bread,
wine and hunger . . . the Gospels are *about* hungers. It's
not a metaphor when Jesus feeds his people."

I heard a mosquito in my ear and gazed up at the sun.
Carrie was looking at me quite intensely, though I was not
in the mood to return her look.

"The body and the spirit must be fed," she insisted. "And
when they aren't, hungers appear and are plugged in the
wrong way. Cigarettes, dope, acid, all the rest of it. People
will put anything in their mouths."

"Communion wafers?" I asked.

"That's bread," she argued, poking at the ground with
her finger, "and I need it. If I were God, I wouldn't need
God, I'd *be* Him. Most of the time He's not inside me, or

He fades away. I have to reach out and take Him in. I feel it mentally and spiritually. I guess that I feel it sexually, too."

Arthur turned away, momentarily biting a fingernail. He looked as though he didn't want to be there, in the presence of this conversation that flew and swooped above his head like an angered bird. Would Christ be at this picnic if Arthur weren't sterile and Carrie's mother hadn't been an alcoholic? Are any effects explained by causes? While I mused about this, she asked me if I wanted any more for lunch, and, when I nodded, she walked toward the house.

"She's sliding toward Christ," Arthur muttered.

"She's there now."

"Moving toward," he repeated. "Not there yet. She thinks it's a food and I think it's a drug. She's still a junkie who only shoots up on weekends. She gets to be all smiles, like after a rush. She says Christ wants me, too, though for what I'm not sure. Maybe for a sunbeam, or to hold his spear and give him a shave. Anyhow, it worries me."

"I know a few people who are getting into Jesus," I told him.

"Yeah? What are they like?"

"Burned and fried from too much tripping, mostly. Groundless. Suddenly they zap into Him. No churches. They don't want mediation, they want it straight, and when they get what they want they're full of energy and color. They sing and dance like they're on 'American Bandstand.' But they all seem dazed to me. They're drowning with the meaning of everything, and everything *has* meaning. Like the Redcrosse Knight in *The Faerie Queene* when he—"

"—Who?" Carrie asked, having suddenly reappeared. With one hand she was carrying a plate of cheese, and with the other she was stroking my hair. I looked up and saw a smile on her face that seemed too brilliant. I felt energy coming in through her hand.

"I have to admit it," I said. "You're plugged into *something*. And as for the Redcrosse Knight, he was given a vision of heaven and the kingdom of God."

"What happened to him then?" she asked.
"Totally immobilized. And then immediately attacked."

From now on I drop out of this essay. After another two days, during which time I did more farming and thought longingly of the agonies of my dissertation—my hands ached for footnotes and dirt!—after having I Cor. 8 read to me while Arthur was gone for an hour in the truck to get fence wire, after some good feelings but mostly the sensation that the power lines in their relationship would be hit by lightning; after all this, in short, I escaped. I felt threatened. I wanted to hear the rest of the story from a distance; I did not want to be a character in it, and I did not want the story to convert me.

Arthur and Carrie had many visitors. They had had almost twenty before I came, and a young man with a Chinese beard and bib overalls arrived a few hours before I left. All through the Midwest, all over the country for that matter, there were and still are networks of farms, communes, *stations*, really, organized and owned by freaks, ex-freaks, dropouts, revolutionaries, teachers, and poets on the run. They all know about many of the others. Lists started, and addresses circulated. All that Arthur and Carrie asked of their visitors was that they help out in the day-to-day work and not stay longer than ten days.

A variety pack: Arthur told me that they saw some "interesting" people. A famous radical who had planted a bomb in an ROTC armory in Kentucky arrived. He found his groove in shelling peas and spent two afternoons dropping the little spheres into buckets and staring at the horizon while he talked about his father's business (selling lawn furniture). They had a fourteen-year-old girl who had hitchhiked there, and who was a veteran of drug-rehabilitation programs, not because she had been an addict, but because she loved the attention she received whenever she said she was hooked. Married couples came. They put up a bearded ex-professor of English who lectured them on D. H. Lawrence's *The Rainbow*. He had credibility because he looked much like Lawrence and groaned loudly in his sleep. One boy of indeterminate age arrived, said nothing at all, and after five days turned catatonic. They took him to the door of the public hospital in Rhinelander and left him there. All kinds, and most of them enjoyed singing about Jesus with Carrie.

Troublemakers? "A true radical has nothing to fear from a stranger."

Months later, a new arrival. Arthur wrote me, "We had a new visitor tonight. I hear this noise in the middle of my sleep, a noise in the barn, and I figure we got trouble or a guest. So I get up and go out there. The barn's dark, of course, I can't see anything, so I say 'Howdy' to whatever's there. 'Yeah' comes back out of the darkness, plus this cough. The man says, 'Over here.' I walk to where I hear his voice coming from until I feel where he is, and I give the hand a grasp. Hairy. He asks if he can sleep there and I say yes. Meanwhile he lights up a cigarette and I see a moment of his face, which I don't like at all. I tell him he can sleep in our living room but if he's going to sleep in the barn he better put out that smoke. 'Yeah,' he says and I see two spit-covered fingers snuff the coal. He tells me he wants to sleep in the barn. I ask him who he is. I am Xavier, he says, then starts up this shitty cigarette cough again. 'I heard about you and your wife and your farm here.' From where, I ask. 'From prayers,' he says. Then, like he owns the place, he says, 'Is that enough? Can I go to sleep now? I'm wrecked, man. Okay?' I tell him sure and go back into the house. He's the first person we've had here who makes me nervous down to my footsoles. I tell Carrie this, and she tells me to relax. But I can't relax, so I get up, sit down here, and I start writing this letter, o lucky man, to you."

The rest of the story I am reconstructing from what Arthur told me.

Next morning, as Arthur pulled some bread out of the icebox, Xavier appeared in the kitchen. He wore a filthy tie-dyed tank top and pants that had been shredded, patched, and repatched. Across the man's chest were hung chains, animal teeth, and beads; one gold earring looped through his left lobe like a tiny doorknocker. His shoulders had a light pelt of hair; on his left arm was a tattoo of a hot-air balloon, and on the right was a full-color tattoo of Jesus Christ on the cross. Arthur sucked in his breath.

"Scared you, man?" Xavier asked.

"No."

"I dig silent entrances. Listen, man, you got any chow? My guts are about tore out with the famine."

Arthur gave him breakfast and explained the rules of the farm. The visitor listened in silence, and, when Arthur was finished, Xavier looked up and asked, "Where's your wife, man?"

"Outside in the garden. Why?"

"Because, man, she been broadcasting prayers all over the country, and, like, here I am. I been a receiving station for ever so long, gettin' those hot beams, y'know? I got something for her."

"What?"

"The Word, man. I got it here in my pocket."

"Carrie, this is Xavier."

She stood up and brushed the dirt off her blouse. After she turned, her eyes locked into his, and she held out her hand. "Hi," she said. "Where are you coming from?" It was a Zen question, the kind she favored.

"Sister, I came out of Them so I could come here to You. I worked my way out of There so's I could be Here. Heard all about Carrie, yes I did."

"You heard? Where?"

"Scars all over my body tell me where to go. Even get messages from the night sweats. I mean, that's the whole story right there."

As if to prove it, Xavier took off his shirt. Six scar lines ran up and down, sideways, or crisscrossed, like a map of the constellations. "And I got one here," he said, lifting his head to point under his beard to his throat, where a light straight scar ran on his neck from behind the ear to down

near his chest. "We was in a patrol when we got am-
bushed. Most of the men, they got killed, but on account
of I was the highest-ranking, VC took me in. Fuckers wanted
information, figgered they could scare it out of me. So they
slit my throat, but light, you understand, not into the big
cables. Just on the surface so the sap would run all over the
floor like I was a virgin or something. Lurps rescued me.
Anyhow, these scars here got news for me, always telling
me shit, and they was the ones that led me straight to you.
Can you dig that?"

Arthur and Carrie said nothing.

"But you know how I really heard about you?" He smiled.
"The loudest voice I got. Him." He pointed to the Jesus
tattoo. "That one," Xavier chuckled, "that Jesus, he sure is
one big blabbermouth."

The visitor said he would help out. Arthur, tentative with
what he thought was a borderliner, said that most of the
work around the farm involved minor tasks, like cutting
thistles or picking beans.

"Whatja want cut?"

Arthur pointed to a back hill. "Thistles up there I got to
get out before the state finds them and takes them out for
me. If they do that I got to pay them."

"Got it," Xavier said, heading for the barn.

"I'll get you a scythe."

"Forget it, man," Xavier said. "I got just the knife for the
job. A souvenir, man, of the bad times, and I got plenty of
those. A blade for every situation, yessir, a cutting tool to
divide down the world."

"I don't like him," Arthur told Carrie that night, in bed.
"I know he's a victim of the war but I also think he likes it.
The changes he's been through have knocked his head over."

"That's true," Carrie said. "But I don't think it matters."

As it turned out, Xavier worked hard: he spent two days
cutting down the mass of thistles, snip snip snip, making
horrible coughing noises in the hot sun. During his break,
he asked Arthur to do him a favor. "Let me speak tonight.

I want to give a sermon." Arthur said he could once the
kitchen was cleaned up after dinner.

Xavier speaking: "People wonder what a dude like myself
has to do with God, with Jesus. They tell me I am profane,
and that's cool, I can accept the criticism because I *am* coming from there, and I gotta work with those feelings. Like
for example I am violent. I like to bust heads. Like once I
was in a bowling alley and some shit started pointing at me
and my earring and my beard, he and his buddy laughing
in this half-assed way, so you know what? I took the fucking bowling ball, man, and I wound up and threw it good,
got the dude right in the loading zone. Gave him a surprise. And a heart attack, if I'm lucky. I walked out of there.
But you understand: violence is spiritual, right? You remember when Christ was up on the cross, man, the smoke
coming out of his ears? Opening up the earth, setting down
those earthquakes? I mean, he was a violent person and
got pissed off easy.

"People don't, you know, remember that he was into
teaching courage to face the elements, and, uh, that's more
than just bad weather, you understand, taking power into
the soul, and not jerking off when the odds are against
you, but facing up to the worst side, death and fire and
windstorms and tornadoes that blast it all apart! Hurricane
Jesus. Did you know *The Wizard of Oz* is all about Him?
Damn straight. I can explain it all: the dog, the brick road,
the whole operation. Got it down cold. I can even explain
these papers."

Xavier pointed to the cigarette papers he used, the Zig-
Zag pack with the bearded man on the outside.

"That's Jesus there, man, having a smoke. Most people
don't realize it's Him on a pack of these papers, but that's
where you got to get the power, man, through the images
wherever they are. You got to whip into Christ and his types
where you can find them, not be too picky, like in these
papers or comic books and the Bible when you need that.
I'm talking power now, right? Batman, for example. I mean,
Batman is all right and I *have admired* Batman, but if you
look at him you'll see what a commercial version of Jesus

he is. This is also true for Superman and the Hulk. If you'll read Paul's letter to the Colossians, you'll see he knew all about Batman and the Hulk, and he really put them down. The less than terrific superheroes, I mean. Put them down. Hit them with lead pipe and then hung them up to dry." Etc.

"Sure, he's a psychopath," Carrie admitted.
"Then why do you want to sleep with him?"
She paused. "I want . . . to put my fingers on whatever is producing all that heat. I want to touch that furnace."
"You'll be burned."
"I'll be changed."

In any man who has taken femininity into himself, love expands to fill all the vacant spaces in the psyche, and if these vacancies predominate, constant love is necessary to prevent emotional hemorrhaging. Arthur began to discover, as his wife slowly left him, moved her spirit and body away, that he had lived off her love as a fuel, a constant condition. He began to feel orphaned and childlike, as if several ribs had been pulled out of his side and he had shrunk. Staring up at the ceiling, alone at night in the bed, he wondered whether he would ever be able to make a decision—water flowed down his cheeks—*any* decision without her help. He felt weeds growing in the gaps she had opened. He heard the visitor yelling and coughing in the barn with his wife. Then the image of Jesus materialized in his head: Jesus up there on the cross, bleeding and suffocating. How the mind resorts to trash when the self is miserable, he thought.

At other times, Xavier wandered across the fields to a small creek half a mile to the south, where he undressed, sat down in the water, and stared up at the sky while grabbing pebbles from the creek bottom and dropping them on his legs. He heard the water talking to his scars, and the scars answering. When he returned, his lips were blue, the color of gas flames.

Another interlude: when Arthur realized his marriage
was breaking up, that he was being cheated out of it by a
madman, he took a special interest in Carrie's image, and
she in his. He told me that one afternoon, just before a
thunderstorm, when the air was completely still and muggy,
smelling of cut grass, he found himself inside the screen
porch, looking through the door at his wife, who stood
outside. She turned and looked in at him. In silence they
gazed at one another as if the screen were a mirror and
they were studying themselves. They examined the eyes
and faces they thought they knew—what, in the configu-
ration of those images, had they loved? They drew very
close on either side. There was a feeling of warmth, deso-
lation, and distance between them. Arthur thinks that he
stood there for at least thirty minutes, his eyes fixed on his
wife, and he can't remember who was the first to turn away.

But she did come up to his bedroom one last time, while
he was taking a nap after lunch. She rattled his shoulders
with her hands in tight fists, and he awoke staring into her
face, where there was a green snake painted on her forehead by Xavier. She uncoiled her fingers and brought them
to the side of his beard.

"Wake up for a minute," she said.

"I am awake." He looked at her. "What are you doing
here?"

"I wanted you to know what it's like."

"Where's Xavier?"

"He's out." She almost tried to laugh. "He . . . he says
he gives sermons to the trees. I think that's where he is
now."

"But that's not what you came to tell me."

"No." She took her hands away from his face. Suddenly
she stood up and her body became as stiff as a piece of
lumber. "Oh God, it's awful being in the same room with
him. Look!" She unbuttoned her shirt and showed him a
black and blue mark on her shoulder. "He hits me, Artie,
when I say something bad. He says he has to punish me
and only the flesh can learn what the tongue has betrayed.

Or something like that. He never hits me in the face. He never hits me where it'll show."

Arthur took her hand. "Sit down." She did. "As soon as he gets back, I'll kill him."

"How?" she asked. "We don't have any guns, remember? And he does. And he has knives. You can't beat him in a knife fight. Besides, I don't want you to kill him. You don't understand. I can't leave him now."

"I *don't* understand. What are you talking about?"

"He makes me crazy, Artie. When I'm around him, I'm just not *there* anymore. It's like being pulled up against the body of an angel, and feeling all of your skin burning, like you've been pressed against a furnace. He's got me seeing things. I almost saw a chariot in the sky yesterday. Almost. I almost saw it. And I can almost talk in tongues. I can understand him when *he* does it. When he makes love . . . "

"Don't tell me."

"They didn't tell me love would ever be like this!" she shouted at him. Then her voice dropped down to a normal level. "They never said it would be insane. I pray to Christ to help me out of this, but, when I see Christ in my prayers, he looks like Xavier. There's no one to help me now. No one."

"Come on, Carrie. Let's get in the truck and just drive away from here."

"No. No. I can't do that. I've explained to you. We were only married, but now this—this is *real*. It just happens to be Hell. And it's crazy. But God," and here she laughed, "it's historic."

"You and I were only married?"

"I suppose I loved you. Somehow. The way I loved toys at the five-and-dime when I was a kid. That way."

"What's Hell like?" He was sitting up, staring at her.

"That's the incredible thing," she said. "You *know* it's Hell when you realize that you can't start to explain it. That's why no one ever describes it. The place is soundproof. That's how I know I'm in it. I can't pray, I can't talk about it, I can't even talk to myself about it. He's nailed my tongue into my mouth. And the sky clears, and the birds fly across it, and

this place is the same it always was, but now it's got eyes
and I'm turning into letters and they scream all night in my
sleep and when he makes love to me, Artie, I swear it, I fall
into the sea and I'm God with my right arm cut off."
    "You'd better leave now." Then he added, "For good."
    "Yes." She bent down to kiss him, and the snake on her
forehead covered his right eye.

    Carrie couldn't quite bring herself to leave, so Xavier tried
to set fire to the house. Arthur was asleep, in a dream of
benign anarchy, taking deep, unpleasant breaths. In the
dream the men were scratching their heads and wondering
who or what was giving off that bad smell. An elder pointed
toward Arthur. He said slowly, with the deliberation of age,
"You should wake up now. This lazy dream is not for you."
Arthur's eyes opened obediently—he loved the elder—but
the stench remained; it grew stronger, and as it did he realized that he was smelling oil and smoke.
    Downstairs, to the kitchen, where he saw the flames
straining up from the soaked rags on the floor, touching
the cabinets with light brushes, then moving away, catch-
ing an empty Spic-and-Span box and, given a breath, rising
toward the table, the legs already on fire. For some reason
he noticed a ripe tomato hissing in the flames, little seeds
dribbling out of slits popped open by the heat. Thirty little
flames climbed the straws of a broom, and nearby flames
jumped in and out of a can of grease. Arthur grabbed an
old pail in the side closet, filled it with water, his eyes burned
to the retinas by the smoke, and threw the water blindly
on his kitchen floor. Snake hisses. He ran the tap into the
pail again and put teakettles and saucepans under the flow
so he wouldn't lose time. Then he flung the water at the
table, the broom, and the floor, and with each toss the fire
hissed again at him, fluttered, and began to gasp, leaving
behind smoke that made him gag. He continued pouring
what he could over the floor and furniture until he could
pick up the rags with a shovel and take them outside. Where
was Carrie? He vomited into the kitchen sink and managed
to walk upstairs. She wasn't there. He looked outside. In

the moonlight he saw Xavier standing in the middle of the driveway, scratching his beard meditatively. "Where's Carrie?" "In the barn, sleeping," he coughed. Then as Arthur watched, Xavier unzipped his fly and took a long slow piss on the road, the stream of water making an almost flatulent sound as it struck the dirt. Xavier gazed back at Arthur with a thin, dull smile.

"You're going," Arthur called. "Now."
"I'm off, man, I'm already gone." Xavier said, zipping up his trousers again. "But you realize she's coming with me."
"I can't stop her."
"Damn straight you can't. You just tits on a bull to her now. Ain't nothing going to grow in her from you, man. You just a seed package with no insides. You're bad ground, buddy, you got no rain and no crops. This here farm is Hopeless Acres, it's where you kids went off to die. I've seen your kind before, man, and you know what? I saw 'em all shot down or cut up or their bodies blown into pieces the size of penny bubblegum with mines and that other sour shit. I lived through that on account of God wanted me to procreate with that woman. And now, me and her are going to mate and make it, our own little baby superhero. Scars told me and that's what she wants. You got lucky with the fire, man," Xavier said, turning around. "You didn't get so lucky with her."

They left together. Arthur did not see them go. He drove away from the farm and visited his friends, just as they had visited him. He came to see me in Buffalo, two weeks before my dissertation defense. Telling the story, he talked half the night, a great actor, playing all the parts. Then, two hours after I had gone to bed, I heard him start to groan, the groans breaking up into smaller sobs, and then out of it, the product, one long wretched stream of vowels.

He has never spoken about Carrie except to say that she had her baby, a boy, and had been arrested somewhere for shoplifting. Xavier left her after the birth, his job completed; she works as a secretary in Los Angeles and puts

the baby in day-care centers. I don't know about her faith,
but I did get a postcard from her once, which said, "Have
been walking around the neurological webs. Please tell them
that it's all right. Do you know how much fright can be
tolerated, day after day?"

I think it's strangely egotistical to send a postcard like
that with no return address.

A year later, Arthur asked to visit me again, but that time
I sent him a confused, abrasive letter, full of petty resent-
ments I had stored up during the years of our friendship.
The letter couldn't say what I felt: that I still loved him, but
that he had been touched by bad luck on a grand scale,
and I didn't want to get within a mile of him. Then he called.
I swore at him over the telephone. I called him a bullshit
artist. At last I admitted that I was frightened of him.

I almost heard him smiling over the phone. He said he
didn't blame me, that he understood how it was, and that
from now on we would only correspond. After my wife
and I were married, he sent me a note of congratulations,
and in the postscript he asked me if I could write up his
story as a sort of disguised essay. Arthur, here it is. I hope
you're grateful.

He should be. He got what he wanted: a farm, peace,
quiet, and a friend who sends him books like *Loose Change*
whenever he wants them. And Carrie got what she wanted,
too: a baby, and a vision of God, or at least part of him. But
it's like a fairy tale. They forgot to tell the angel *exactly* how
they wanted their wish to come true. As Arthur said to me,
"I ordered the whole dinner, and they brought it to me.
The only trouble was, it was spoiled. And I still had to
eat it."

He says he doesn't make any more wishes. There are
certain jackpots no one wants to hit twice. As for me, I am
writing this from the second story of a brick house in a nice
neighborhood. There's a garden outside my window. I spend
time with academics; I don't know any pushers now, and I
don't keep a stash. If Saint Jerome himself were to knock at
my door this very instant, his head ringed with heavenly

fire and his eyes burning with the fever of a truth he knows and which I have acknowledged my entire adult life, I am reasonably certain that I would glance once, recognize him, and turn him away from my door, whose threshold I could not bear to see him cross, without another word.

The Model

"You're so pretty," Naomi says, sitting at the kitchen table, while she watches Carter doing the dishes, wearing only his undershirt. Carter taps one foot on the tile in time to hidden body rhythms. Naomi stares patiently at the foot, the ankle, the calf, the thigh, the curve of the buttocks. "You're so pretty," she repeats, "it's mean for you to be a faggot."

Carter is a very good dishwasher: attentive, scrupulous, gentle with glass but rough on soiled baking pans. His slow arm and wrist movements betray his sensual feeling for soap. He rinses carefully. The drying dishes sparkle in the aftermath of his attention.

"I'm here," he says.

The kitchen window has a view of the street. If anyone cared to look in, that person would see Carter bent over the hot water in the sink. The possibility that someone might see him does not apparently bother him. Finishing up, he starts to sweat: his forehead, chest, and underarms. He takes off his shirt, throwing it to the floor next to his feet. Naomi groans. She cannot get up to embrace him because Carter doesn't like to be touched by women except in bed, and then only in certain preprogrammed ways.

"Once every four weeks?" she asks. "For a few hours? That's being here?"

He turns around, the full display. "So tell me never to come back." He smiles ironically, a seller's-market smile. "Tell me to get lost."

Naomi picks up the coffee cup, carries it over to Carter, and holds it to his mouth, so that he can sip before drying his hands.

"You smell of Naomi," Mel says at the door when Carter gets back. "Chanel No. 5 and that other thing she wears."

"It isn't Chanel No. 5. It's something she got from the Avon lady. Also she has a lot of deodorants. Stuff like Tickle

and Dry Idea. They take up most of the room in the medi-
cine cabinet." Carter sits down on the sofa. It is three in the
morning and Mel is in his bathrobe. "Oh, Mel," he says.
"I was worried about you."
"I left you a note."
"Where? Where did you leave me a note?"
"On top of the TV."
"I didn't see it. I looked by the phone and there was
nothing there. When you go off like that, I watch Johnny
Carson, but I don't laugh. I always think you're in an accident or something."
"Mel, you always think I'm with Naomi. And it's so unusual, it's almost like never."
"It isn't like never. It's like sometimes."
Mel looks down at Carter, whose arms are flung out at
the top of the sofa and whose head is thrown back in mock
despair. Carter yawns. "I came back," he says. "I always
come back."
"You *won't* always come back." Mel walks over to Carter
and takes his hand. "Someday," Mel says, "someone's going
to kidnap you and keep you in a cage, just so he can look
at you." He laughs. "I'd do it, but it's illegal. I bet Naomi is
like that. I can imagine."
"She adores me. She stares at me a lot. I kind of like it."
"No kidding," Mel says. He is tracing out Carter's fingers.
"Is the candle lit?" Carter asks. He means the bedroom
candle, which adds erotic atmosphere and lessens his fear
of the dark.
"I've had it on all night," Mel says, "for when you got
home."

While Carter stands with his back to the life studies class
at the art school, Naomi sketches him, standing twenty feet
away. She works patiently on proportion, shading, and details of musculature. She is conscious of the other students'
eyes on Carter, conscious of Carter's vague pleasure in being
looked at, and his ultimate indifference. Her teacher, Mr.
Dunham, materializes next to her easel, holding his head
up to see her work through his bifocals.
"You got the backbone wrong down here," he says,

pointing. "You got the arc exaggerated. And you got the
vertebrae highlighted too much. This is like a billboard.
Look at these shoulders." He moves closer to her. "You been
sleeping with this guy?"

Naomi nods. "Sometimes. When he lets me."

The professor snickers sympathetically. "You should know
better," he half-whispers. "Beautiful women are bad, but
beautiful men are the scourge of God. Get a straight arrow,
kid, I'm telling you. A beer drinker."

He walks away, while Naomi stares at Carter's back.

Mel has fed the parrot, the fish, the birds, and the snakes,
closed up the pet store, and is driving home. On the way
he listens to Ravel on the car tape machine. The music makes
him think of Carter, which is why he listens to it. The piece
is *Daphnis and Chloe*. The music is beautiful and doesn't seem
to care about anything, even when it gets excited. It can
rise to a climax and still be bored. This sort of beauty and
self-sufficiency doesn't make Mel cry, as has happened in
the past with his other lovers. It's as if the world doesn't
touch Carter at all. A bomb could go off, leaving him indifferent. "Nothing hurts you," Mel says aloud, to Ravel and
the car. "Nothing gets to you."

Carter is out. He is not at Naomi's, nor at home. He is
downtown, getting his exercise by taking long walks through
the department stores. He likes to start at luggage, then
move on to sleepwear, lingerie, leather goods, men's wear,
notions, and jewelry, the department where without fail he
always ends up. He keeps moving, taking additional steps
on the escalator. Today he has tried on but not purchased
a J. Press powder blue suit, a leather jacket imported from
Spain, cordovan shoes from French Shriner, a silk tie, and
a pair of dark glasses. Clerks are always glad to have Carter
around: he makes the merchandise look good. Right now
he is in lingerie. Carter is staring at a black negligee. Its
complicated system of frills confuses him momentarily: he
cannot exactly see the purpose in it. Naomi wears either
pajamas or nothing, and his encounters with other women

have been too brief to shed much light on the purposes of sleepwear.

"Yes?" A saleslady.

"I was looking," Carter says, never embarrassed.

The saleslady surreptitiously glances down at Carter's ring finger, then looks up. "A gift for her?"

"Yes," Carter says absently.

"It's very attractive, isn't it? What size is she?"

"Size?" Carter tries to picture Naomi. It's very difficult: he closes his eyes.

"Well, small or medium, for example?"

"Medium. She's a medium."

The saleslady nods. Scenes like this are common. Carter stands transfixed, staring at the mannequin's breasts, that strange purposeless shape. Carter is a technician of clothes, but this time he is stumped. He stares. "How much?" he finally asks.

The saleslady tells him. "And I can giftwrap it."

"No," Carter says with force. "Just in a box." Then he changes his mind. "On second thought, giftwrap it, would you?"

"Yes, sir. A card?"

"What?" He shakes his head. "No. No card."

He does not give in to his temptation to buy her a pair— a very small pair—of gold hoop earrings. On the way out, he finds a public phone and calls Naomi, just to let her know he's coming.

Naomi is sitting at the kitchen table, giving English lessons to Klaus, when the phone rings. Naomi knows German and these lessons help meet expenses. Klaus, however, has a receding hairline, wears Hawaiian shirts, and walks with a stoop. No one would be tempted to draw him. But he does bring over Rhine wines and sing German folk songs to her, deeply moved by her presence. After the call, she walks over to Klaus and holds her hand down for a shake.

"The time is up, Klaus. Now you must go."

"But the lesson." He taps his watch. "It is not over yet."

Naomi taps her own watch. "It *is* over." Klaus's face takes
on an overdisciplined look. In German she says, "But nat-
urally we will see each other next week."

This promise, in his native tongue, softens him somewhat, and he heads for the door. "Next week," he says, "I
will be so eloquent, you will not stop me early."

"Sorry, Klaus. It's somebody special."

He nods sadly, closing the door behind him.

Carter knocks on the door and opens it simultaneously.
Naomi's temptation is always to run over to him and put
her arms around him, but Carter will not permit it. Instead, she stands back. In Carter's hand is a gift: his first.
Tissue paper and red ribbon, ending in a bow.

"What's this?" she asks.

"A thing I brought you."

She opens it. When she sees it, she is too stunned even
to laugh. Taking it out of the box, she holds it up. It is
daring in all the conventional ways. At last she laughs. "Jesus Christ," she says.

"I want to see you in it."

"Why?"

"I don't know." He gazes at her. It is hard for her to meet
or to resist his lizard's eyes. "I just do. Here's what I think
I want. I want you to go into the bedroom and put this on.
Pull the shades. That'll be dark enough. Then tell me when
you're ready."

"Carter," she says. "This isn't like you."

"I know. Would you put it on?"

Carter takes off his clothes in the hallway and waits for
her. At last she says she's ready, and he walks in. She lies
on the bed with a faintly hopeful look. Carter looks at Naomi in her negligee and crosses his arms.

"I don't get it," he says.

"It's supposed to be pretty."

"It isn't. It's just weird."

"Don't say that."

"But it is. It's just sort of silly."

"You've got to be straight to like it."

"I guess. Maybe you should take it off."

"Okay." She turns her back to Carter. When she is naked she turns toward him. He is looking at her with the same puzzled expression. "Now come here."

He lies on the bed and Naomi touches him in the places where he has said she can. When he is somewhat aroused, she says, "You're a picture."

"I know."

"Tell me you like me," she says. "Say I'm pretty."

"How can I?" he says. "I shouldn't be here."

"Be really funny. Give us both a laugh. Say that you love me."

"Oh sure. Yeah. Right. I love you." He coughs. "Now let's get this over with."

Carter has fallen asleep. Now, in the light of the bedside lamp, Naomi is gazing at what she adores and what humiliates her, the sleeping physical presence of Carter. She puts on her clothes and walks over to her dresser. One by one she takes the bottles down and carries them, three in each hand, to where his body lies. She lines them up. She opens the bottle of Wind Song and dabs it on his left instep, ankle, and calf. For the other leg she uses Aviance. Carter groans, turns his head, but does not wake. Taking a long breath, Naomi now opens a bottle of Nocturnes, a gift from her ex-fiancé, and spreads it on his waist. For his back, L'air du temps, and for his neck and shoulders, Bal à Versailles. That does it. Naomi gags, goes to the bathroom to wash her hands, and clicks off the light. The room is pitch dark, with the curtains pulled and the shades down. She leaves the apartment with the perfume bottles neatly lined up on the dresser.

Once, carelessly, Carter had given Naomi his phone number, and she calls it now from an all-night McDonald's. It rings one and a half times before Mel answers.

"Hello," Naomi says. "This is Naomi. We haven't met."

"I know who you are. Is it Carter? Is he all right?"

"He's fine. He's at my place and he's asleep. I'm not calling from there. I decided to go out for a walk. But anyway,

I was sort of wondering if you'd give him a call and wake him up. I'm kind of angry at him and I'd like him to be gone when I get back."

"Okay," Mel says.

"Thanks."

"Carter isn't easy, is he?"

"No."

"Well, thanks for calling."

"Sure."

The telephone: sharp cardiac shock, its call, pulling Carter by the hair out of sleep into this room, pitch dark, that smells like an overturned garbage can. He stares into the dark, having forgotten his name and where he is, and he feels for a moment the darkness staring back at him, pressing him deeply into its blanket. Where is the phone? Where is the light? Where is *she*? He reaches over to the other side of the bed and feels the negligee. He stands, trying to see anything, and holds his arms out, doing his best to remember where the phone is stashed. "Naomi?" He has remembered her name. "Naomi?" He will not shout. "It's the phone." It rings and rings and rings. What is that smell? It does not occur to Carter that it originates with him. Stumbling like a sleepwalker he makes his way down the hall toward the kitchen, where the telephone is shrieking. Though Carter can just make out where the thing is, the darkness follows him. He knows it's behind him. It's always there: it has this habit.

"Hello?"

"Carter. Get home. She wants you out. She's not there. She called."

"Mel."

"Don't stop for a beer. Don't do anything. Just come home."

"She called you? Where is she?"

"She said she wasn't there. She's out. What did you do to her?"

Carter is too sleepy to think. "I gave her a pair of black pajamas."

"Oh Jesus. You're crazy! Get dressed and get your ass home."

"All right." Carter has a little-boy voice. This is it. "All right, Mel. I'll be there."

He dresses in the light of the bedside lamp. The sickening smell in the air will not go away. He decides to disobey Mel and stop at a bar for a beer.

Mel sits up, waiting for Carter. This is an old scene for him and he has devised many different strategies for dealing with it: dope, Cole Porter, Ravel, bourbon, cigarettes, Johnny Carson, Tom Snyder, David Letterman, call-in radio shows, ham sandwiches, and pizza, but finally nothing can compete with staring out the window at the lights of the city. There is this sentence Mel likes to say to himself, when he knows no one is in the room and can hear him. The sentence is, "There are people who are worse off than I am." He can say it as often as twelve times in a row, and, when he does, he visualizes the poor, the hungry, and the sick. Immediately he feels better, and, although he does not believe in God, he thanks Him all the same. It is raining tonight, and he imagines the bums sleeping on sidewalks, in the rain, under newspapers. After three-quarters of an hour, he begins to think that Carter has done something stupid, like stopping in one of those bars he likes, where the gay crowd is weirder than Mel can sometimes believe. Even worse, Carter sometimes risks straight bars, because he likes to shoot pool. After two hours, Mel can no longer stare out of the window. He gets up and begins to pace, and though he does not believe in God, he is now praying. He prays that Carter will come home any minute now, unhurt, looking the way he usually does, like a gift, like all the colors of the rainbow.

Horace and Margaret's Fifty-second

A few months after she had put her husband, all memory gone, into the home, she herself woke one morning with an unfamiliar sun shining through a window she hadn't remembered was there. A new window! Pranksters were playing a shabby joke on her. She rose heavily from the bed, a groan bursting by accident out of her throat, and shuffled to the new window they had installed during the night. Through the dusty glass she saw the apartment's ragged backyard of cement and weeds. A puddle had formed in the alley, and a brown bird was flapping in it, making muddy waves as it bathed. Then she looked more closely and saw that the bird was lying on its side.

"I remember this view," she said to herself. "It's not a new window. I just forgot to pull down the shade." She did so now, blocking the sun, which seemed to her more grayish-blue than it had for years. She coughed rhythmically with every other step to the bathroom.

It was Tuesday, and their anniversary. He would forget, as usual. Now, in his vacancy, he had stopped using shaving cream and razor blades. He tore photographs out of their expensive frames, folded them into baskets, and used them as ashtrays. He took cigarette lighters to pieces to see how they worked and left their tiny wet parts scattered all over his nightstand. He refused to read, claiming that what she brought him was dull trash, but she had suspected for a long time that he had forgotten both the meaning of the words and how to read them from left to right across the page. She didn't want to buy him cigarettes (in his dotage, he had secretly and then quite openly taken up smoking Chesterfields again). He lost clothes or put them on backward or declared universal birthdays so he could give everything he owned to strangers. The previous Wednesday, she had asked him what he would want for their upcoming anniversary, their fifty-second. "Light bulbs," he said, giving her an unpleasantly sly look. She glanced at his lamp and saw that the shade was pleated oddly. "They give you plenty of bulbs here," she said. "Ask them." He shook his head for thirty seconds before he replied. "Wrong bulbs," he said. "It's the special ones I need, with the flames."

"Light bulbs don't have flames," she said. "It's filaments now."

"Don't argue with me. I know what I want. Light bulbs."

She was at the breakfast table reading the paper when she remembered that she had dropped an egg into the frypan, where, even at this moment, it must still be frying: hard, angry, and dry. She forgave herself, because she had been thinking about how to get to the First Christian Residence before lunch, and which purple bus she should take. She walked to the little four-burner stove with its cracked oven window, closed her eyes against the smoke, picked up the frypan using a worn potholder with a picture of a cow on it, and dropped her last egg into the wastebasket's brown paper bag. Now she had nothing to eat but toast. She was trying to remember what she had done with the bread when she heard the phone ring and she saw from the kitchen clock that it was 10:30, two hours later than she had thought.

She picked the receiver angrily off the wall. "Yes," she said. She no longer said "Hello"; she was tired of that.

"Hello?"

"Yes," she said. "Yes, yes, yes, who it it?"

"It's me," the voice said. "Happy anniversary."

Very familiar, this woman's voice. "Thank you," Margaret said. "It's our fifty-second."

"I know," the voice told her. "I just wish I could be there."

"So do I," Margaret said, a thin electrical charge of panic spreading over her. "I wish you could be here to keep me company. How are you?"

"Just fine. Jerry's out of town, but of course David's with
me, and last night we roasted marshmallows and made a
big bowl of popcorn."

David. Oh yes: her grandchild. This must be David's
mother. "Penny," she said.

"What?"

"I just wanted to say your name."

"Why?"

"Because," Margaret said carelessly, "because I just
thought of it."

"Mother, are you all right?"

"Just fine, dear. I'm going to take the bus to see your
father in half an hour's time. I'm going to wish him a happy
anniversary. I doubt he'll notice. He won't remember it's
our anniversary, I don't think. Maybe he won't remember
me. You can never tell." She laughed. "As he says, the
moving men just come and take it all away. You can't tell
about anything. For example, I thought they put a new
window in my room last night, but I'd only forgotten to
pull down the window shade." She noticed a list on the
refrigerator, a list of things she must do today. It was getting late. "Good-bye, Penny," she said, before hanging up.
She picked the list off the refrigerator and put it in her pocket.
Then she stood in the middle of the room, her mind whirling and utterly blank, while she stared at the faucet on the
right-hand side of the sink and, above it, attached to the
cabinet, a faded color photograph of a brown-haired girl,
looking away from the camera toward a tree. It was probably Penny, when young.

Once Margaret was on the bus, she was sure that everything would be fine. The sun was out and several children
were playing their peculiar games on the sidewalk, smack-
ing each other and rolling over to play dead. Why weren't
they in school? She knew better than to ask children to
explain their reasons for being in any one spot. If you asked
such questions, they always had that look ready.

The bus was practically empty. All the passengers, thank
God, seemed to be respectable taxpayers: a gentleman with

several strands of attractive gray hair sat two rows in front of her, comforting her with his presence. The sun, now yellow, was shining fiercely on Margaret's side of the bus, its ferocity tempered by tinted glass. Margaret felt the sun on her face and said, "Sweet sweet sweet sweet sweet tea." This, her one and only phrase to express joy, she had picked up in 1935, from a newspaper article that had tried to make fun of Gertrude Stein. The article had quoted one of her poems, and Margaret had remembered its first line ever since. "Sweet sweet sweet sweet sweet tea," she said again, gazing out the window at obscurely sinister trees, with far too many leaves, all of them the wrong shape.

Horace, before he had been deposited in the First Christian Residence, had been a great one for trees: after they had bought a house, he had planted them in the backyard, trimmed them, fed them, watered them when droughts dusted their leaves. "Trees," he liked to say, "give back more than they take. Fruit, oxygen, and shade. And for this they expect no gratitude." He would have been happy working in a nursery or a greenhouse. As it was, he worked in a bank, and never talked about exactly what he did there. "It's boring," he would say. "You don't want to hear about it." Margaret agreed; she didn't. Only toward the end had he raged against the nature of his work. But he didn't shout at Margaret; he told the trees. He told them how money had gobbled up his life. He talked about waste and cash, and he wept into his hands. Margaret watched him from the kitchen window. She watched him as he lost his memory and began to give names to the trees: Esther, Jonas, Ezekiel, Isaiah. He told Margaret that trees should have serious, adult names. For eighteen months now, he had confused the names of his trees with the names of his children. He wanted his trees to come visit him in the home. "Bring in Esther," he would say. "I want to see her." Because of this, Margaret no longer gazed at trunks, branches, or leaves with any special pleasure.

She remembered where to get off the bus and was about to go into the residence when she realized that she had no anniversary present. She stood motionless on the sidewalk. "He won't remember," she said aloud. "What's the difference?" She waited a moment and found that she disagreed with her own assessment. "It does make a difference. He'll think I'm making it up if I don't bring him something." She looked around. At the corner there was a small grocery store with a large red Coca-Cola sign over its door. "I'll go down there," she said.

The store was darker than it should have been and was crowded with confusing teenagers. Margaret found herself looking at peanut-butter labels and long rows of lunch meat. Then she was in front of the cash register, holding two Hershey bars. "I'll buy these," she said to the coarse girl with the brown ponytail and the pimples. She was already far down the street when she realized that she hadn't waited for change, or a bag to put the chocolate in. It was the first time she had given him a present she hadn't wrapped.

Holding the candy bars and her purse in one hand, she opened the large front door of the First Christian Residence with the other. This was the worst moment, because of the smell. Margaret knew that oldsters couldn't always keep themselves clean and tidy, but their smell offended her nevertheless. Just inside, a man with wild hair and a bruise on his forehead, whose eyes were an angelic blue, smiled at her and followed her in his wheelchair as she walked to the elevator. A yellow Have-a-nice-day sticker, with a smile face, was glued to the back of the chair.

"Beautiful day, Margaret. Don't you agree?"

"Yes." This man had been pestering her for months. He was forward, and looked at her with an old man's dry yearning. "Yes," she repeated, inside the elevator, as she pressed the button for the third floor, wanting the door to close, "it is indeed a nice day. You should get outside into the sunshine for some fresh air and vitamin D, instead of staying in here all the time."

He wheeled himself onto the elevator and turned around

so he was next to her. "I stayed," he said, "because I was hoping you'd come." The elevator doors closed, at last. "I can still walk, you know. This chair is a convenience." Margaret tried to sound chilly. "I'm going to see Horace, my husband. I don't have time for you."

"Horace won't miss you. His memory's bad. He remembers the 1945 World Series better than he remembers you. Let's go for a walk."

"No, thank you." She remembered his name. "No, thank you, Mr. Bartlett."

"It's Jim. Not 'Mr. Bartlett.' Jim." He smiled. She noticed again his remarkable eyes. The numbers above the doors flashed. It was the slowest elevator she'd ever been on, slow to prevent shocks to the elderly.

"This is my stop," she said, backing out into the hallway once the doors opened. As they closed again, Mr. Bartlett leaned back in his wheelchair and gave her a bold look.

Horace was in his room, wearing a Wayne State University sweatshirt, gray corduroys, and tennis shoes. He was watching "The Price Is Right" and eagerly smoking a Chesterfield when Margaret came in. He glanced at her and then went back to the activity of the contestants. On screen, a woman in uniform was spinning a huge, multicolored wheel, and the studio audience was roaring, but Horace failed to share the excitement and watched the television set indifferently. Margaret picked up a newspaper from the chair by the window and arranged the flowerpots on the sill.

"Good morning, dear," she said. "How did you sleep?"

Horace didn't answer. Perhaps it would be one of those days. Lately he had been retreating into silence. Apparently he found it comforting. Margaret clucked, shook her head, and walked over to the television set, which she turned off.

"It's our anniversary," she said. "I don't want daytime television on our anniversary."

On the table next to Horace was a breakfast roll. A fly walked back and forth on it, as if on sentry duty. Margaret picked up the plate and took it out to the hallway, placing it on the floor next to the wall. When she came back, Horace was still staring at the dark television screen.

She gazed at him for a moment. Then she said brightly, "Do you remember Mrs. Silverman, two floors up in the building, Horace? The apartment building? Where we moved after we sold the house? Mrs. Silverman, whose husband was so terribly bald? I'm sure you do. Well, anyway, several nights ago there was a great commotion, and it seemed that Mrs. Silverman was reading the paper, probably just the want ads, as she did usually, when she had one of those seizures of hers. She knocked over a tall glass of ginger ale. It left a stain on the rug, I think. They came for her and took her to the hospital, but the word in the building is that it may be curtains for Mrs. Silverman."

"The moving men," Horace rasped.

"Yes, Horace, the moving men. Someone in the building called for them. Sometimes they can help and other times they can't. You are looking very scruffy today, Horace," she said. "Where did you get that awful sweatshirt?"

"Someone gave it to me," he said, avoiding eye contact.

"Who?" she asked. "Not that horrid little Mr. List?"

"Maybe." Horace shrugged.

"I'd think you'd be ashamed to be in that sweatshirt. You were never a student at Wayne State. Never. You went to Oberlin."

"It's warm," Horace said. "And it's green."

"Which reminds me," Margaret announced, "that I thought they had put a new window into our bedroom last night. But I just forgot to pull down the shade. Oh. Someone called this morning." She thought for a moment. "Penny." She waited for him to show recognition, but he kept his face turned away from hers. "She called to wish us a happy anniversary. It's our anniversary today, Horace."

"I know that," he said. "I know that very well."

"Well, I'm glad. I brought you something."

"Light bulbs?"

"No. Not light bulbs. I explained to you about the light bulbs. You don't need them. What do you need them for?"

"Bliss," Horace said.

"For bliss? I doubt it. No. Well, what I brought you was this." She handed him the Hershey bars. "Happy anniversary, dear. These were the best I could do. I am sorry. Age has brought us low. I would have presented you with a plant in the old days."

"These *are* the old days," Horace said. He gazed down at the dark-brown wrappers. "Thank you. Mr. List likes chocolate. So do I, but Mr. List likes chocolate more than I do." Horace suddenly looked at her, and she flinched. "How's Penny? And where's Isaiah?"

"Penny's fine. She toasted marshmallows with David last night. And Isaiah's lost his leaves because it's late October."

Horace nodded. He appeared to think for a long time. Then he said, "I went out yesterday. I wanted to drop something on the ground the way the trees do. Dead leaves reactivate the soil, you know. They don't rake leaves in the forest, only in the suburbs. It's against nature and fool-hardy to rake leaves. I pulled out a strand of my hair and left it in the grass. Why did we get married in October? Tell me again." He smirked at her. "I've forgotten. I've lost my memory."

"It was 1930, Horace. Times were hard. When you finally secured a job at the Farmers and Mechanics' Bank, I agreed to marry you."

"Yes."

Margaret knew she had made a serious mistake as soon as she saw the tears: she had mentioned the bank.

"When did you stop kissing me?" Horace asked.

"What?"

"After the war. You wouldn't kiss me after the war. Why not?"

"I think this is very unpleasant, Horace. I don't know what you're talking about."

"Of course you do. You wouldn't kiss me after the war. Why?"

"You know very well," she said.

"Tell me again," Horace said. "I've lost my memory."

"I didn't like it," she muttered, standing up to look out of the window.

"What didn't you like?"

"I didn't like the way you kissed me."

"We weren't old yet," Horace said. "It's what adults do. They have passions. You can't fool me about that."

Margaret felt tired and hungry. She wished she hadn't taken the breakfast roll out to the hallway.

"I'm not here to settle old scores," she said. "Do you want to split one of these candy bars?" Outside, a blue convertible with a white-canvas roof came to a stop at an intersection and seemed unable to move, and all around it the small pedestrians froze into timeless attitudes, and the sun blinked on and off, as if a boy were flipping a wall switch.

Horace struck a kitchen match on the zipper of his pants and lit up a cigarette. "I love cigarettes," he said. "I get ideas from the smoke. Call me crazy if you want to, but yesterday I was thinking about how few decisions in my life were truly important. I didn't decide about the war and I didn't decide to drop the bomb. They didn't ask me about nuclear generators, or, for that matter, about coal generators. I had opinions. They could have asked me. But they didn't. Mr. List and I were discussing this yesterday. The only thing they ever asked us was what we were going to do on the weekends. That's all. 'What are you doing Saturday night?' That's the only question I can remember."

Margaret tore the brown paper away from the candy bar, then crumpled up the inner wrapper before she snapped off four little squares of the chocolate. Someone seemed to be flicking lights inside the First Christian Residence as well. The taste of the chocolate rushed across her tongue, straight from heaven.

"Want any rum?" Horace asked. "I have some in the closet. Mr. List brought it for me. On days like this, I take to the rum with a fierce joy." This line sounded like, and was, one of his favorites.

"Horace, you can't have liquor in here! You'll be expelled!"

Suddenly he appeared not to hear her. His face lost its color, and she could tell he would probably not say another word for the rest of the morning. She took the opportunity to snap off one more piece of the chocolate and to straighten

the room, to put smelly ashtrays, pens, shirts, and dulled
pencils in their rightful place. There were pencil sketches
of trees, which she stacked into a neat pile. In this mess
she noticed a photograph of the two of them together,
young, sitting under a large chandelier, smiling fixedly.
Where was that? Margaret couldn't remember. Another
photo showed Natwick, Horace's dog in the 1950s, under
a tree, his mouth open and his dirty retriever's teeth prom-
inent. Horace had trained him to smile on cue.

"Someday, Horace," Margaret said, "you'll remember to
keep your valuables and to throw away the trash. You've
got the whole thing backward." Seeing that he said nothing, she went on. "So often I myself have . . . so often I,
too, have found that I have been myself in a place where I
have found myself so often in a place where I have found
myself." Standing there, squarely in the middle of the room,
she felt herself tipping toward Horace's cigarette smoke,
falling through it, tumbling as if off a building, end over
end, floor after floor. Horace held his hand up. Margaret,
whose mind was still plunging, walked toward him. He
whirled his hand counterclockwise as an invitation to bring
her ear down to his mouth.

"Don't tell me anything," he whispered. "That's for kids.
And be quiet. Listen. There's a bird scratching in the tree
outside. Hear it?"

She did not. Margaret bent down to kiss his forehead
and made her way out of the room, sick with vertigo. The
hallway stretched and shrank while she balanced herself
like a tightrope walker in a forward progress to the elevator. Three floors down, Mr. Bartlett was waiting for her,
wearing a cap and a jacket in his wheelchair, but she tot-
tered past him, out into the sun, which she saw had turned
a sickly blue.

There was something wrong with the bus.

She sat near the back. The bus would start, reach twenty-
five miles an hour, then stop. Not slow down. Stop. In
midair, as it were. When it stopped, so did the world. The
trees, pedestrians, and birds froze in midair, the birds glued

to the sky. And when this occurred, Margaret grabbed the
top of the seat in front of her, pressing it hard with her
thumbs, hoping she could restart the world again.

She looked up. In front of her a little girl was kneeling
on the plastic seat next to her mother, facing the back, staring at Margaret. The little girl had two pigtails of brown
hair, a bright-red coat, and round-rimmed glasses too large
for her face. As the bus began to move, Margaret stared at
the girl, frowning because she wanted the youngster to know
that staring is rude, a sign of bad breeding. But as she
scowled and frowned, and the bus passengers swayed like
a chorus together, she was horrified to feel her own eyes
producing tears, which would run partway down her cheeks
and then stop, as the bus itself stopped, as time halted.
The little girl reminded Margaret of someone, someone she
would never exactly remember again.

The girl's mouth opened slightly. Her eyes widened, and
now she, too, was crying. Her glasses magnified her tears,
which were caught by the rims in tiny pools. Margaret
gathered herself together. It was one thing to cry herself
for no special reason. It was quite another to make a little
girl cry. That was contagion, and a mistake in anyone's part
of the world. So Margaret wiped her eyes with her coat
sleeve and smiled fiercely at the girl, even laughing now,
the laugh sounding like the yip of a small dog. *"Toujours
gai, toujours gai,"* she said, louder than necessary, before
she realized that little girls on buses don't speak French
and would never have heard of archy and mehitabel even
if they did. "There's a dance in the old dame yet," Margaret
said, to finish the phrase, quietly and to herself. She drew
herself up and looked serious, as if she were on her way to
someplace. She was not about to be cried at on a public bus
in broad daylight.

"What a nice day!" Margaret said aloud, but no one turned
toward her. The little girl took off her glasses, wiped her
eyes on her mother's coat, and gave Margaret a hostile look
before turning around. "The old lady shows her mettle,"
Margaret continued, editorializing to herself, simultaneously making a mental note not to engage in private con-
versations where other people could hear her. It takes a

minimum of sixty years' experience to recognize how useful and necessary talking to oneself actually is. When you're young, it just seems like a crazy habit. Margaret did not speak these thoughts aloud, as the bus whirled upside down and righted itself; she whispered them.

They went past a world of details. Sidewalks broke into spiderweb patterns. A green squirt gun was in a boy's hand, but the bus was moving too quickly for her to see the rest of the boy. In a tree that she noticed by accident, a brown bird flew out of a nest. Something redbreast. Robin redbreast. The bus driver's head, suddenly in the way of the sun, shone a fine gunmetal blue. On a jungle gym, a boy wearing a green sweatshirt, smaller than Horace's, hung down from a steel bar with only his legs, his knees, holding him there. Margaret stared at him. How was it possible for a human being to hang by his knees from a bar? More important, why would anyone want to do it? Before an answer came, the boy faded out and was replaced by another detail, of a sea gull standing proudly in someone's alley, an arrogant look on its face. The sea gull cheered Margaret. She admired its pluck. The other details she saw were less invigorating: an old man, very white in all respects, asleep in a doorway; two young people, across the street from the art institute, kissing underneath a tree (the tree and the kissing made her flesh crawl); and now, at last, a cumulating, bright-pink, puffing cloud of smoke exploding out of someone's back yard, someone's shed, on fire or dynamited, even the smell reaching her. The bus drove on and Margaret forgot about it.

She remembered her stop, however, and was halfway up the sidewalk when she remembered that she had forgotten to get out at the Safeway to buy groceries. She counted all her canned goods, in her mind's eye. "I'll be all right," she said, "and besides, there are more buses going here and there. It's their fate in life." She trudged on into the building.

Skinny Mr. Fletcher, employee of the United States Postal Service, had already come and gone with his Santa's sack of bills and messages. Margaret unlocked her mailbox, hoping for a free sample of a new soap. Instead, there was

a solitary postcard inside, showing on its picture side Buster
Keaton walking squarely down the middle of a railroad track.
On the other side was a message from Horace, written in
his miserable script. Some letters had been crossed out, but
he had not given up.

> Dear Margaret,
>   Happy littaniversery
>   today
>   from love Horace
>   ps remember lightbulbs

Where had he mailed the message? Where, more important, had he found the stamp? How had he remembered
the address? It was all very mysterious. The postcard was,
of course, simply one of his monstrously large postcard
collection, which he had taken with him to the First Christian Residence, over two hundred of them. He had traded
a few for cigarettes. Margaret looked at Buster Keaton as
she went up the stairs, the stairway extending and short-
ening, like a human-sized accordion.

She opened her door and stepped into the living room.
On the left was her pastel-blue sofa, next to her Emerson
radio and Muntz television set, and on the right was her
mother's harmonium, underneath a mirror. Behind the sofa
were bookshelves, filled with books she and Horace had
read to each other: Robert Benchley, Don Marquis, Brooks
Atkinson. She could remember their names but not the
character of their work. "Feels like I'm walking through
Jell-O," she meant to say, but no sound could make its way
out of her throat.

She stood stranded inside the door, waiting for something to happen. At last the invisible steel wires holding
her feet loosened for a moment, and she managed to get as
far as the harmonium. Then the movie came to a halt again.
She hadn't taken her coat off, nor could she. She was forced
to look at more details: the spiral pattern on her white rug;
the legs of the harmonium; her own white surprised face
in the mirror. "I know where I am," she said. "I'm home."
But she didn't remember the mirror. Who had brought it
here? Had it been delivered by Mr. Fletcher, from his sack?

"I should go to the kitchen," she said. "Or I should take a nap." Step by step, feeling the great work her progress required, she walked to the kitchen, weighted down by the thousands of details that were in her way. A nick in the floor, a jolly afternoon sun, a cookie crumb in the shape of an elf sleeping on the dinner table. A brown lamp with a tiny dial switch on its base, and hundreds of slits in its metal shade. And on the harmonium, photographs. Photographs of her three daughters, and one of herself, Margaret, and her husband, Horace, sitting down beneath a chandelier somewhere, and smiling. In the chandelier were eight light bulbs, their glass transparent, like Mazda bulbs, shaped from a broad base to a sharp tip, like a flame. "Well, I never noticed," she said. "You can't blame me for that."

In the kitchen, she was drinking water when she looked out the window and saw them. They were dressed in uniforms, and they had big arms and big faces. They had their truck in the alley and were carefully loading chairs, lamps, sofas, and tables into it. She noticed that they didn't joke as they took Mrs. Silverman's furniture away, that it was a solemn event, like running up a flag. Feeling foolish and annoyed, Margaret cranked open the window and began to shout. "Who told you boys to come here? Where do you think you're taking those things?" She noticed a lion painted on the side of the moving van and was momentarily disconcerted. "I hope you boys know what you're doing!" she shouted at last, down to the large, astonished faces. When they finally looked away from her, she lifted the glass of water to them, drank, then spilled out the rest into the sink.

She tried to remember what she had planned to eat for either lunch or dinner and found her way back into the living room, where she sat down in front of the television set. She saw, reflected in the dark screen, herself, in black-and-white, miniaturized. She smiled and laughed at the tricks television could play, whether on or off. And then, behind her, but also in the background of the set, she saw a tree, waiting for her. Horace had left his trees behind when she and he had moved out of the house. She stood up and went to the window again, and with the clatter of furniture being hauled away in the alley serving as a background, she began to stare at the branches and dried leaves of the one tree the management had planted, and then she began to talk. She told the tree about Horace. Then she laughed and said that she and he would probably sit together again, checking on the sun and the other tricks of light shining from odd directions on the open gulf lying radiant and bare between them.

The Cliff

On the way out to the cliff, the old man kept one hand on the wheel. He smoked with the other hand. The inside of the car smelled of wine and cigarette ashes. He coughed constantly. His voice sounded like a version of the cough. "I used to smoke Camels unfiltered," he told the boy. The dirt road, rutted, dipped hard, and the car bounced. "But I switched brands. Camels interfered with my eating. I couldn't taste what the Duchess cooked up. Meat, salad, Jell-O: it all tasted the same. So I went to low tar. You don't smoke, do you, boy?"

The boy stared at the road and shook his head.

"Not after what I've taught you, I hope not. You got to keep the body pure for the stuff we're doing."

"You don't keep it pure," the boy said.

"I don't have to. It's *been* pure. And, like I say, nobody is ever pure twice."

The California pines seemed brittle and did not sway as they drove past. The boy thought he could hear the crash of the waves in front of them. "Are we almost there?"

"Kind of impatient, aren't you?" the old man said, suppressing his cough. "Look, boy, I told you a hundred times: you got to train your will to do this. You get impatient, and you—"

"—I know, I know. 'You die.'" The boy was wearing a jacket and a New York Mets cap. "I know all that. You taught me. I'm only asking if we're there yet."

"You got a woman, boy?" The old man looked suspicious. "You got a woman?"

"I'm only fifteen," the boy said nervously.

"That's not too old for it, especially around here."

"I've been kissed," the boy said. "Is that the ocean?"

"That's her," the old man said. "Sometimes I think I know everything about you, and then sometimes I don't think I know anything. I hate to take chances like this. You could

be hiding something out on me. The magic's no damn good
if you're hiding something out on me."

"It'll be good," the boy said, seeing the long line of blue
water through the trees. He pulled the visor down lower,
so he wouldn't squint. "It'll be real good."

"Faith, hope, charity, and love," the old man recited. "And
the spells. Now I admit I have fallen from the path of righ-
teousness at times. But I never forget the spells. You forget
them, you die."

"I would not forget them," the boy said.

"You better not be lying to me. You been thieving, sleeping with whores, you been carrying on in the bad way, well,
we'll find out soon enough." He stopped the car at a clear-
ing. He turned the key off in the ignition and reached under
his seat for a wine bottle. His hands were shaking. The old
man unscrewed the cap and took a long swig. He recapped
it and breathed out the sweet aroma in the boy's direction.
"Something for my nerves," he said. "I don't do this every-
day."

"You don't believe in the spells anymore," the boy said.

"I *am* the spells," the old man shouted. "I invented them.
I just hate to see a fresh kid like you crash on the rocks on
account of *you* don't believe in them."

"Don't worry," the boy said. "Don't worry about me."

They got out of the car together, and the old man reached
around into the backseat for his coil of rope.

"I don't need it," the boy said. "I don't need the rope."

"Kid, we do it my way or we don't do it."

The boy took off his shoes. His bare feet stepped over
pine needles and stones. He was wearing faded blue jeans
and a sweatshirt, with a stain from the old man's wine bottle
on it. He had taken off his jacket in the car, but he was still
wearing the cap. They walked over a stretch of burnt grass
and came to the edge of the cliff.

"Look at those sea gulls down there," the old man pointed,
"Must be a hundred." His voice was trembling with nervousness.

"I know about the sea gulls." The boy had to raise his
voice to be heard above the surf. "I've seen them."

"You're so smart, huh?" the old man coughed. He drew

a cigarette out of his shirt and lit it with his Zippo lighter. "All right, I'm tired of telling you what to do, Mr. Know-it-all. Take off the sweatshirt." The boy took it off. "Now make a circle in the dirt."

"With what?"

"With your foot."

"There isn't any dirt."

"Do like I tell you."

The boy extended his foot and drew a magic circle around himself. It could not be seen, but he knew it was there.

"Now look out at the horizon and tell it what I told you to tell it."

The boy did as he was told.

"Now take this rope, take this end." The old man handed it to him. "God, I don't know sometimes." The old man bent down for another swig of wine. "Is your mind clear?"

"Yeah," the boy said.

"Are you scared?"

"Naw."

"Do you see anybody?"

"Nope."

"You got any last questions?"

"Do I hold my arms out?"

"They do that in the Soviet Union," the old man said, "but they also do it sitting on pigs. That's the kind of people they are. You don't have to hold your arms out. Are you ready? Jump!"

The boy felt the edge of the cliff with his feet, jumped, and felt the magic and the horizon lifting him up and then out over the water, his body parallel to the ground. He took it into his mind to swoop down toward the cliffs, and then to veer away suddenly, and whatever he thought, he did. At first he held on to the rope, but even the old man could see that it was unnecessary, and reeled it in. In his jeans and cap, the boy lifted himself upward, then dove down toward the sea gulls, then just as easily lifted himself up again, rushing over the old man's head before flying out over the water.

He shouted with happiness.

The old man reached down again for his wine.

"The sun!" the old man shouted. "The ocean! The land! That's how to do it!" And he laughed suddenly, his cough all gone. "The sky!" he said at last.

The boy flew in great soaring circles. He tumbled in the air, dove, flipped, and sailed. His eyes were dazzled with the blue also, and like the old man he smelled the sea salt.

But of course he was a teenager. He was grateful to the old man for teaching him the spells. But this—the cliffs, the sea, the blue sky, and the sweet wine—this was the old man's style, not his. He loved the old man for sharing the spells. He would think of him always, for that.

But even as he flew, he was getting ideas. It isn't the style of teenagers to fly in broad daylight, on sunny days, even in California. What the boy wanted was something else: to fly low, near the ground, in the cities, speeding in smooth arcs between the buildings, late at night. Very late: at the time the girls are hanging up their clothes and sighing, sighing out their windows to the stagnant air, as the clocks strike midnight. The idea of the pig interested the boy. He grinned far down at the old man, who waved, who had long ago forgotten the dirty purposes of flight.

A Short Course in Nietzschean Ethics

In his discussion of the Superman, Nietzsche fails to address several problems. For example: what should the Superman be called? In America, the name *Zarathustra* has only comic effect. Would Nietzsche have liked the name *Waldo Steiner*? Might it have been appropriate for the world-transcendent being announced by Nietzsche's prophet? Waldo Steiner certainly thought so. In his diary, which he once handed to me, he wrote, "It is first necessary to overcome the self before one can overcome others. One cannot eradicate weakness without particular attention to the uses of fright. The strong man improves himself by means of *the essential fact of his fear.*" He permitted me to read these dictatorial words in the belief that I would be impressed by their terribleness. This misjudgment was utterly characteristic of him.

For a few years, Waldo Steiner lived unburdened by fright, playing as he did the role of the boy next door to me, in a neighborhood puffed by Realtors as "modest and charming." Living so close to Waldo was not much of a problem, since our ages compared favorably, and, though I could hit a baseball much farther than he could, he had the better pitching arm. Big deal, *I* made the scores, not Waldo, and just because he was all-city Peewee League pitcher in 1958 doesn't mean that I bear him a grudge.

Despite his fine pitching arm, Waldo was a creep, in a particularly technical sense of that term. This behavioral problem, this creepiness, had a reasonable cause: his mother had died under somewhat mysterious circumstances when Waldo was nine. I always thought that God had taken Mrs. Steiner away after a stroke and coma, but perhaps it was nerves, pills, and alcohol, as so many people said. In any case, after she joined the angels, Waldo bought a telescope, a slide rule, and began shamelessly to cheat at checkers and Monopoly, taking advantage of his shocking loss.

"You cheated," I announced harshly one day. "You *put* that card at the top of the Community Chest pile. I saw you."

"Liar. I did not either cheat." Fury stoked up behind his glasses. "You always say that when you start to lose."

"That's because you've been cheating so much lately."

He had already mastered the trick of bending his head and looking at me from the tops of his eyes, as preachers do. "Okay," he said, "if you think I cheated, we won't play. It's my game." He started to put his play money back into the slots of the Monopoly bank, money I had planned on getting honestly if he ever landed on Pennsylvania Avenue, where my solitary red plastic hotel stood.

"Quit it," I said. "Take your get-out-of-jail-free card, if you want it so much." And I mumbled, "To cheat for it."

"I heard that," he said, picking up the board and throwing it across the room so that it hit the shelves where his toy racing cars were arranged. The cannon, his piece, and the ship, mine, went flying and landed miraculously in a catcher's mitt lying on his desk. "You wreck everything!" he shouted at me. "You think you're so good. You think . . . " and he paused to imagine what I thought. "You think that I'll do anything to win. That's only 'cause you *always* lose. Since my mom died you always say I cheat."

"That's creepy, Waldo," I said, strangely feeling the impulse to hit him immediately after he had mentioned his mother. "I don't do that. Even when you do cheat. Like now."

"Boys?" Waldo's father called from the living room, where he was rattling his evening paper. "Is everything all right?"

"Sure, Dad," Waldo shouted. Then he turned to me. "I know your secret," he whispered. "You think that because you can hit a baseball so far that you're hot stuff. Well, you don't impress me."

"I can beat you up any time," I whispered back, "you hamburger."

"Who's a hamburger? I'd like to see you try," he said, his fists clenched. "I'm so tired of you living next door to me. With all the people in the world, I have to get you. Why don't you just move away? And why don't you start by going home?"

I did go home and did move away, eventually, to college, followed by Waldo, with whom I shared an apartment. If he was a creep, he was *my* creep, with his dirty sweaters, seedy mustache, worn jeans, and omnipresent slide rule. He liked to lie on the sofa, holding his book up in the air as he read it, making comments to me, to our girlfriends, to the walls.

Sample: "Chekhov sucks."

"That shows how ignorant you are," I said, looking up from a math problem. "Chekhov is a very great writer."

"All right. Listen to this very great writing. 'When we are dead, men will fly in balloons, change the fashion of their coats, but life will remain the same, full of mysteries and happiness. In a thousand years men will sigh just the same, "Ah, how hard life is."' What trash."

"It's not trash, it's true."

"It's weak-kneed and spineless," he said from his sofa, cigarette butts and empty beer bottles lined up on the floor around him like toy soldiers on guard. "And it's tiresome. In this play, everyone is always sighing. They're like tires with air leaking out. I'd like to shoot them. God bless the Russian Revolution! It put an end to this stuff. In a thousand years," he continued, fixing his stare on me, "no one anywhere will sigh. It'll be outlawed. And so will this play. This play perpetuates weakness."

"Speaking of weakness," I interrupted, throwing my failed proof into the wastebasket, "are you going to baseball practice this weekend?"

"Is it optional?"

"Yeah."

"Then I'm not going. I'm trying to move in on that girl in my sociology class, Sheila Carlson. Remember her? If I make any progress," he sighed, "I'm going down to the river with her."

"Sheila Carlson," I said, doodling. "I don't remember any Sheila Carlson. What's she like?"

"To start with, she's funny. She makes very sly remarks. She's not just another piece of toast. And she has the body of a fine violin. I asked around, and I heard that she's guarding her virtue." He did his best to leer. "But I plan on turning her into a slut."

"I don't see what these girls see in you," I said. "Why can't they guess what your true character is?"

He held up a beer bottle to the light, burped, and then drank. Doing his best General Jack D. Ripper imitation from *Dr. Strangelove*, he said, "Women sense my power."

Early Saturday afternoon, Waldo brought Sheila back to the apartment. He was carrying a blanket to which leaves and twigs still clung, and she was holding onto a paper bag full of trash. Her eyes had that sleepy look. She glanced once at me.

"You must be William," she slurred, stumbling over the carpet as she made her way into the kitchen to dump the garbage under the sink, before returning to the corner where I sat in my sweatclothes. I had followed baseball practice with a brief catnap.

"You're Sheila, right?"

"Yeah." She looked around. "You boys," she said. "You always live in such filth and squalor." She sniffed. "And you give off a bad smell. Why is that?"

"I've been playing baseball," I said. "I sweat when I exercise."

"Don't you shower?"

"When I want to."

"Don't you care what inferences people draw from the odors you give off?"

"What people?"

"Well, me, for example."

"I thought you'd be down at the river huffing and puffing with Waldo." I pointed at her clothes. "You *have* been huffing and puffing with Waldo, haven't you? You're hardly one to talk." In spite of myself, I smiled at her. "By the way, where *is* Waldo?"

"In the bathroom, I guess," she said, "Why?"

"Just wondered."

"You just wondered," and now she was smiling. "What are you grinning at?"

"I don't know." Perhaps my odor was vanishing. "*You're* the one who's smiling."

"The tawdriness of your room amuses me, and so does the . . . well, let's call it an aroma, and leave it at that."

"Are you asking me to take a shower?"

"I'll think about it." She went to the window and looked out. "Wait until Waldo is gone."

"You turncoat," Waldo growled over his coffee, into which he was pouring spoon after spoon of sugar. This was a month later. "You took away my woman. My trust in you was ill-conceived. I have it figured out, dated to the exact day. You made your move when I was helpless in the bathroom, didn't you?"

I shrugged.

"*I* took her down to the river," he almost shouted. "I started this romance, and I was the one who snowed her. Now she's saying that she loves you and other things of that nature. What a turnaround: I've been traded in on you, like an old car. This puts an end to our friendship, you thief. You stole her away. You stole my baby." He slurped mournfully at his coffee.

"Don't be maudlin," I said. "Oh, incidentally. Our lease is up next month. I want to move out. I want an apartment by myself."

"Heap it on, traitor." He looked over his glasses at me. "Yes, I saw this coming, too. Betray your childhood friend and steal his woman and then move out—oh, it's like a terrible comedy, isn't it, and me as the butt of the joke. You're undoubtedly the worst longtime friend I've ever had. Listen, pal, I know why Sheila walked out on me. Don't flatter yourself that it was your wit or your body, because I know better."

"What was it?"

"It's because I have dark hair."

"Waldo, nobody in the world cares that you have dark hair. I don't think Sheila even *noticed* your hair. It's because of your other qualities that she gave you up for me. Your creepiness, for example. Certain attributes that *only you* possess."

"Such as?"

"You cheat at cards and you drink too much beer. You belch and pass gas, and you have an inflated opinion of your potential. Women have a way of not liking such things."

"No." He shook his head sadly. "It's because I have dark features. She wanted a paleface. Women do, you know. Blond on blonde. Her genes went ape in the presence of your genes, and that's the entire history of the world right there."

"There are a million women," I said, "alive right now, today, who would care for you deeply if you only made a minimal effort to be a gentleman, to be ingratiating, to stand up straight."

"It isn't manners they go for," Waldo smiled. "It's fear."

Eventually I married Sheila. We remained happy as long as I was in graduate school studying Racine. We lived on my fellowship and starved romantically, but when I was unable to find a job after receiving my degree, starvation seemed less romantic. Since we now had a child, I had to take some quick action. I borrowed money from my parents and tried to start a business. It failed. A seedy department store with creaky wooden floors hired me as a clerk. With agony and terrible effort, I tried to struggle up into the comfort of the middle class, fighting off debt and despair on each step. The shouting in our house occasionally did wake the neighbors, but we stopped short of being a public nuisance, Sheila and I. The department store promoted me: now I was in charge of luggage. Then they moved me to personnel. Amassing some investment money again, I tried another business, and, though it did not exactly succeed, it didn't exactly fail. The middle class finally gathered me to its breast, and I wanted no more. We paid our mortgage on time and gave dinner parties at which the guests discussed politics and property taxes. With these curious household gods gathered around me, I slowly became my house and my neighborhood, and adult life settled down to its numbered routines.

I had become so normal that I had almost forgotten about Waldo. We telephoned one another at times after college, but Waldo disliked it when Sheila answered, and of course writing letters was just out of the question for him. So as I struggled into a life of harmlessness, I assumed that Waldo was doing the same.

One night, after Sheila and our child were asleep, the phone rang; when I picked it up, the receiver barked in my ear. "Chadwick? It's Waldo." A local call.

"Waldo? Where are you? Are you in town?"

"Yes, I'm in town. I'm in room 435 of the Dorchester Hotel. I thought I would call you. It seemed the thing to do." He let the pauses slip in. "Do you mind?" His gargoyle voice rose in intensity. "I certainly wouldn't want to keep you up."

"Keep me up? No, no." Now *I* waited. "Waldo, what the hell are you doing here in town?"

"I'm here on business," he said unhelpfully. "Interviews." He paused. "Things." I thought if he became more vague he would have to stop using words. We both waited. "Well," he said, "what are you going to do?"

"What do you mean, what am I going to do?"

"I mean," he said, with next-door irritability, "are you going to invite me over for a beer, or are you going to come down to the hotel and have a drink here, or are you just going to hang up?" To my surprise, he then laughed. I had never enjoyed Waldo's laughter, and I didn't care for it now.

"Oh," I said, "I guess I'll come down and get you. I just want to know something. Are we friends? Are you mad at me or something?"

"Naw. Come and see me. Get me out of this hotel. Give me a chance." He sounded like a carnival barker. "After all, I've known you for decades, and that must count for *something*, right?"

"Okay, Waldo. I'll be there in half an hour. I'll drive by the front door."

"What kind of a car do you have?"

"A Buick," I said.
"I thought so."

He stood, slightly bent, in the hotel's doorway, peering
out at the traffic with a stale, sour expression, and upon
seeing him I thought of Ernest Hemingway's slanderous
description of Wyndham Lewis: Lewis, Hemingway had
said, looked like an "unsuccessful rapist." When Waldo
spotted me, and I honked, he rushed out, his raincoat flapping and his hands reaching toward the doorhandle like
mechanical claws.

"I wasn't sure you'd come," he said, shaking my hand
reluctantly. "I had my doubts."

"Hi, Waldo," I said. "You're looking . . . pretty well." His
hand *felt* like a mechanical claw. "Good to see you." I was
shocked to see how his hairline had receded, and I didn't
like the sickly ocher shade of his skin. "So tell me," I said,
"what've you been up to?"

"Listen," he said, "before we get into that, there's something I want to ask you." In the dark of the car, with only
the dashboard light and the streetlamps illuminating his
face, he was looking more like a midwestern but stealthy
vampire, eyes peering out into the nighttime traffic for a
quick score. "Are you happy?"

"What?" I could see he was baiting me. "What a dumb
question. Of course I'm happy." I chuckled, giving back
laugh for laugh. "What about you?"

I stopped at a red light, waiting for his answer. After a
minute I knew he wouldn't respond. At last he said, "Where
is Kiernan Hospital?"

"The other side of town," I said. "First Avenue South
and Twenty-fourth Street. Why?"

"Somebody I know is there," he muttered. "Distant relative. My God, this is a dreary place. Why do you live here?"

"Here?" I glanced at the stores, streets, and houses. "This
place is like anywhere else, Waldo. And I like it. It's hard
to go broke in a university town: the students have lots of
money. We're doing all right."

"Selling luggage."

"That's right. Everyone sells something. What do *you* sell?"

"My project in life," he began, "is to survive without being silly. I didn't want . . . " His voice trailed off, as if he were tired. "I didn't want to sell things. I wanted to do something serious. Something fundamental." He waved his hand at the windshield. "There are great forces out there trying to make us do terrible things. I choose not to do them. I have a great loathing for salaried work. I can't stand business. I can't stand capitalism. I bet I'm the only person you know who can say that."

"What do you do?" I asked.

"I've been reading."

"That's your job? What about your family?"

"I have one."

"Children?"

"Two."

"Boys? Girls?"

"Yes."

"Come on, Waldo, I'm just trying here." I waited. "You said you've been reading. What've you been reading?"

"Nietzsche," he said. He looked at me but I decided not to look back. "And I *do* work, you'll be glad to know. With computers. But not exactly on a salary. I'm not a drifter." He slouched down in the car seat. "No, not that."

"Is your work silly?" I asked.

"Not always."

I stopped asking questions and so did he. I wasn't sure whether he was my enemy or not.

When he arrived at my house, he stared up at it and then began coughing, a long chain of horrible liquid hackings like a diesel trying to find the proper gear. "Nice place," he said, finally. "Four bedrooms?"

"Yes."

"Make you happy?"

"What kind of question is that?"

"Sort of question I ask."

"That's kid stuff. Come on, Waldo, this is life. You don't ask people stuff like that when they're grown up."

"Really?"

"Really. How would you like it if I asked you if you loved your wife and your job and your life and all that sort of thing?"

"I wouldn't mind it."

"Like hell you wouldn't." We were sitting there in the car, in the dark driveway, right in front of the garage. I was feeling annoyed. "The point is," I said, "to keep on going. That's the *only* point. A person's got to have some sort of life!" I wasn't quite sure what I was saying, but I knew that whatever it was, it was true. "I don't make judgments about other people."

This last sentence brought on Waldo's diesel hack again for another minute. "*You* don't want to talk about things," he said.

"No, I don't want to talk about things!" I was raising my voice. "Not with you, not with anybody! It's pointless."

"Let's get out and walk," Waldo said. "Let's walk around the block here. That might be interesting."

"In the dark?"

"Your neighborhood," he pointed out, "has streetlights. We'll be all right. Don't you ever take walks?"

"No," I said. "I jog."

"You jog."

"Yes, I jog, goddammit!" I shouted. "Who do you think you are, the grand inquisitor? I jog four miles a day. What's it to you? Listen, if you want to take a walk, let's take a walk, but don't let's sit here like a couple of fairies, okay?"

"Anything you say." He opened the door and got out. I thought I saw sweat on his forehead. His breathing was peculiar and shallow. He started walking down the street ahead of me with a sort of short, hopping gait, like a man who has recovered from polio. This, I knew, was a trick: Waldo had never had polio.

I was determined to be polite, to recover my composure and self-control. "So, Waldo," I said, "what's new?" By now I had caught up to him and was trying to walk at a speed that would approximate his.

"Let me tell you a story," he said. "There were these two

friends." He stopped on the sidewalk and smiled at me, as if he had been saving up this malicious parable for months. We had come to a corner, and it struck me that Waldo had wanted an intersection as the setting for his fable, one of those "one man goes down one path, the other man goes down the other path" stories. But then we saw a bus far down at the end of the street, coming toward us with a curious muffled sound. It was the only vehicle in sight. Waldo seemed to forget his story as he watched the bus. There is something eerie about a bus on an empty street at night, with its passengers fully illuminated from the inside; in such light they have a submerged, spectral quality. I realized that we were standing at the bus stop. The bus pulled alongside us, and I looked up as the door opened and the driver stared down at us. "No, no," Waldo said. The driver closed the door and the bus pulled away with its eight hollow-faced riders.

"We're standing," I said, "at the bus stop."

"I know."

"You were going to tell me a story, Waldo. It was about two men."

He was coughing. The bus exhaust had apparently gone into his lungs. "Friends," he said. "Two *friends*."

"So. What's the story?"

He fanned his left hand in the air. "Who cares?" he said. "I'll tell you later. You tell me a story."

"I don't have any stories."

"Not any? Not one story from this whole mass of your life?"

"No. Not one."

"Strange," he said, looking down into the street.

"It's *not* strange! I don't have any stories to tell. I lead a normal life! What's wrong with that? There aren't any stories in normal life and there never have been. You're just trying to see me squirm. You want to hear what I had for dinner? I'll tell you what I had for dinner, but it's not a story. *You* tell a story if you like them so much. *You're* the reader."

"You don't have to get so upset," he said. He was still

hunched over, looking down carefully. At last he seemed to find what he was searching for, grabbed it, and straightened up.

"Waldo," I asked, "why are you holding a rock in your hand?"

"This rock?" He tossed it a few inches in the air and caught it.

"Yes. That rock."

"You don't have any stories. You want one? Here's a rock." He handed it to me.

"What am I supposed to do with this?"

"Well, you could throw it through that window over there." He pointed at the picture window on the corner house, which belonged to a grumpy retiree named Prescott.

"Is this what your friend Nietzsche advises?"

"It's what *I* advise," Waldo said. "Prove to me that you're not an adult."

"What?"

"You heard me. Prove to me you're not an adult. Pretend this is Halloween. Take good aim and haul back and throw that rock through that window. And if you do that," he said quickly, "I'll believe in you again, *even if you miss.*"

"If I break that window—"

"—If you *try* to break that window . . . "

". . . you'll believe in me."

"That's right," Waldo said. "We'll be friends."

"Really?"

"Fucking A."

"No," I said. I tossed the rock into the street.

"Cheap coward middle-class comfort-monger."

"Throwing a rock into plate glass isn't my idea of effective protest."

"What is?"

"Waldo," I said, shouting again, "what do you want out of me?"

He looked at me in the dark. "This will do," he said.

"Come on." I grabbed his coat sleeve. "We're going back to the house. Damn you, you haven't grown up or anything. Listen, I'll make you a cup of coffee and then I'm taking you back to your hotel."

"That's what I thought," Waldo said. "By the way, don't you want to know why I'm in town?"

"Actually," I said, walking quickly, "I *would* like to know."

"Guess."

"Aw, Jesus Christ. I'm supposed to *guess*?"

"Go ahead. Try it. Why am I here in town?"

We were approaching my house, and I was walking fast, from one pool of light to the next on the sidewalk, two or three steps ahead of Waldo and his fake limp. "You're out of a job," I guessed, "and you're here to find one, and you thought I would help. Also, your health is terrible. Am I right?"

"Maybe."

We were at the front door. I was afraid he might grab the knocker and start pounding. "Well, am I right or not?"

"For me to know and for you to find out," Waldo said.

"I don't believe this."

"You need me more than I need you," Waldo informed me.

"Bullshit."

"Who's unemployed? Who's sick?"

"Why did I ever like you?" I grabbed him again, and with my arm crooked behind his back I opened the door and pushed him through into the foyer. He was easy to direct; he put up no resistance at all. "All right," I said, "come in and settle down for a minute." Crossing the living room, I pushed him toward the sofa, and he surveyed the walls as I took off his coat.

"Well, this is nice," he said. "Kind of a *homey* home. That *is* the idea? Yes. Well. Where is she?"

"Who?"

"Your wife. Sheila. Remember?"

"Upstairs, sleeping. Keep your voice down."

"And your son?"

"He's upstairs, too." I had gone beyond calling him out for his obnoxiousness and recognized that I'd made a mistake in allowing him into the house. "Waldo, you get your

cuf of . . . *cup* of coffee and then you go back to the hotel.
You aren't staying here."

He nodded, while his hand reached into his sportcoat's
inner pocket. He pulled out a book, which I thought was
probably a paperback edition of his favorite philosopher,
until I saw its plain gray cover. A notebook. He made quick
notations in it, glancing around the room at our furniture,
pictures, and magazines, his fountain pen scratching hur-
riedly over the paper as if he were an anthropologist. "What
a place," he said. "What a place."

"Do you want some coffee, or not? I'm afraid to ask if
you want cream or sugar."

"Don't be. Yeah, I'll have some the minute I finish writing."

"Is that," I pointed, "your diary?"

"Yes." He turned to another page. "Want to read it?" He
held it up to me. "Read it. Just read what's there on the
page."

Taking the book, I silently examined his handwritten
thoughts. "Read it aloud, why don't you," he said.

"'It is first necessary to overcome the self,'" I read in my
blandest monotone, "'before one can overcome others. One
cannot eradicate weakness without particular attention to
the uses of fright. The strong man improves himself by
means of *the essential fact of his fear.*'" I closed the book and
put it down. "Waldo," I said, "you've been reading too much
G. Gordon Liddy lately. What's all this fear?"

"My fear," he said. Then he shook his head. "You sim-
plify everything. I see that now. You won't understand."
He waited, and a curious expression of boyish trust broke
out onto his face. "May I have that coffee now?" he asked.

"All right."

"The queen of air and darkness," he said, almost to himself. "Where did you say she was?"

"Sheila?" I asked, heading into the kitchen, ignoring the
tone of his question. "She's upstairs. Be quiet, or you'll wake
her."

I take pride in my coffee. For me there is an almost ob-
scene pleasure in making wasteful trips to the specialty store
to choose this month's beans. One learns to enjoy grinding

them, and watching the aromatic powder as it falls into the filter paper's little funnel. Like a child with a chemistry set, I watch the coffee dribble down into the glass beaker, checking its color. Too strong? I add more water if the coffee appears to be muddy. I lost myself in the making of coffee that night, and this attention to detail explains why for a moment I forgot about Waldo, and why, when I came into the living room, he was of course no longer sitting on the sofa.

"Waldo?" I stood there holding two cups of coffee. "Waldo?"

I heard the creak of the floorboards. He was upstairs.

With mad calm, I put the coffee cups down on our Plasticene coasters. Then, stealthily, taking the stairs two at a time, I hurried up to the second floor, where I stood in the hallway and glanced first into our little boy's room. Somehow I knew that Waldo wouldn't be in there, and he wasn't. I hurried toward our bedroom.

The light in the hallway shone through the door's opening and illuminated the bed, on whose edge Waldo was sitting, gazing down at the sleeping face of my wife. I stared at him as he stared at her. Sitting there, looking down at Sheila, Waldo shivered as if a feather touched his back. He shivered a second time, making the bed shudder. His hands came up to cover his eyes. A short bleat came out of him, a lamb's cry, as he began to weep. As the tears struggled down his cheeks, Sheila awoke. She saw him, without surprise. She lay for ten seconds, silently observing his sobs.

"Why, Waldo," she said, her voice full of sensibility and drowsiness. "You're crying." And in one smooth movement she raised her bare white arms to his face.

With that movement, I emerged from my own dream. I am not sure what happened, but I know I ran into the bedroom and virtually picked up my childhood friend, and with a rush I carried or threw him toward the stairs. His legs gave way under him, and he staggered down three stairs on his knees, like a penitent making his way to a monastery altar. I heard my boy cry out, and in that same moment I realized that comical groans were escaping from my own mouth. At the landing, I reached around Waldo's shoulders, picked him up, and carried him down to the main floor, the two of us looking like drunken students at a fraternity party. Putting his diary into his raincoat pocket, I then forced his hands and arms into the sleeves.

"Help me," he said. "Help me help me."

"I'll help you, all right. I'll help you right out the door." And, with the same arm around him, I rushed him through the front entry, through the porch, onto the steps, and down to the sidewalk.

"Willie," he said, "what am I going to do?"

For two seconds, speech left me. Then I said, "Find a cab. If you're so sharp, keep walking until you find one. Just do it." I sneezed. "All right. I'll call the cab company, and I'll tell them you're wandering out here alone. They won't have much trouble finding you. You'll stand out."

"Willie," he repeated, "what am I going to do?"

I moved forward to give him a hug, but stopped. "I'll be damned if I know," I said.

He pulled away. His face was angry. "Let go," he said. "You humiliated me." He turned and began walking down the block. Without looking back, he said, "Call the cab company, will you? A yellow cab—I like them better. There's a good boy."

"Take it easy, Waldo. Good luck."

It's still not clear to me whether Waldo has moved to this town. He may have, either for his health or for a job. I thought I saw him last week on the street, near a bank, but I wouldn't stop to check. I don't like people like Waldo. If he hadn't lived next door to me, I wouldn't have agreed to be his friend. I won't be his friend any more. I certainly hope that he reads this story: it'll fix him. Waldo! Look at yourself here! See how I've humiliated you, in front of all these people!

The Would-be Father

Wiping off the kitchen counter after dinner, Jerome happened to glance at the window over the sink and saw a woman's face outside, peering in. The face had an inquisitive but friendly expression. It belonged to Mrs. Schultz from across the street, who tended to wander around the Heritage Condominium complex in the early evening while under the influence of powerful medications prescribed for her after-dinner and bedtime pains.

"Hi, Mrs. Schultz," Jerome said, waving a sponge. "Are you all right? Do you know where you are?"

"I think so," she said, waving back. Her gray hair was bundled at the top of her head, and the lines around her mouth rose when she smiled. "I think I know where I am, if I'm across the street and if you are who I think you are. I wanted to see that boy of yours. Also, I'm thirsty. Can you pass a glass of water to me through this window?"

"I can't, Mrs. Schultz," Jerome said. Looking boyish and preoccupied, as was usual for him, he pointed at the window. "Screens. And Gregory's already in his pajamas. See how late it's getting?" Mrs. Schultz glanced up, but it was still too early for stars. All the same, she nodded. "Let me take you home." He dried his hands, poured a glass of water, and glanced down the hall. Gregory's door was closed, but Jerome could hear him singing. He carried the water outside to where the old lady stood near the arborvitae, slowly moving her left hand back and forth in the air. Jerome realized that she was trying to brush away gnats. "Here," he said, putting the glass in her other hand. She sipped it, thanked him, and gave it back. Then she took his arm, and together they crossed the street. It was spring: he could hear children playing softball in the distance.

"You said it was late," she said, "but I don't see any stars."

They walked up the sidewalk to her front door, which was wide open, and Jerome turned her around so that they faced his house. He could smell onions, or something acidic, coming from the inside of her condominium, a permanent smell and a sign that she had lost the knack of effective housekeeping.

"The days are longer now, Mrs. Schultz. Daylight savings time. Look over the roof of my garage at the sky. What do you see? Do you see anything?"

"I see a dot," she said.

"That's Mars," Jerome told her, letting out a breath with the word. "The red planet. So you see? It *is* getting dark. I'm leaving you here, okay? You should do yourself a favor and go inside now. Try to get some rest. Will you be all right?" Mrs. Schultz stared at his shirt buttons. "You should try to be all right," he said.

"Oh, it's you I'm worried about, not me," she said. "What a man in your position does, after all. And that dot, Mars. It's right over your house, isn't it? It's not over my house." She looked at him with her I'm-not-so-dumb face. "Thank you anyway. I'll go in now. Say goodnight to that little boy of yours."

"I will."

She turned once more and went in. Jerome watched her trudge down the hall toward the living room chair in front of the perpetually blaring television set. He reached inside her door to make sure the lock was set and then closed it before going back.

Gregory was kneeling at the side of his bed, his arms stretched out over the patchwork quilt, his fingers clasped tightly together. The only illumination in the room came from the Scotty dog night-light, which cast a pale glow on the bed and dresser and made them look like toy furniture used in a circus act. Gregory, who was five years old, was praying to Santa Claus and Mr. Rogers. With his face buried in the quilt, his words broke out with difficulty, a mumble of wishes.

On the opposite side of the room was a narrow rocking chair, next to a low table on which was placed a windup double-decker bus and an ashtray. Above them was a wall poster of Paddington Bear, a poster the boy had outgrown. Jerome's routine was to go into the room, kiss Gregory goodnight, light up a Dutch Masters cigar, and turn on the boy's cassette recorder, which would play the same selection of tunes as always, Glenn Miller's greatest hits, starting with "Moonlight Serenade." When Jerome had been a boy himself, suffering from asthma and unable to sleep, his mother would play Glenn Miller on the table model Magnavox. In this way he became accustomed to falling asleep to the big-band sound.

His prayers finished, the boy climbed into bed and waited for Jerome to tuck him in. He was used to Jerome's cigars and now liked the smell at bedtime. After Jerome entered, he kissed Gregory and, as usual, sat down to be close to the ashtray, before tapping the button on the recorder.

"Where were you?" Gregory asked.

"Mrs. Schultz was over here. I had to help her back across the street." He waited a moment. "Did you say your prayers?"

"Yeah," the boy said. He picked up his stuffed dragon and made a sound.

"Was that a roar," Jerome asked, "or a yawn?"

"He's sleepy," the boy said. "Tell me a story. Tell me a story with me in it. Tell me my horoscope." As always, he tripped over the word. "What's happening tomorrow?"

"Don't you want to hear a bunny story or something?"

"No. My horoscope."

"Okay." Jerome took a deep breath. "The planets are in a good position for you tomorrow, especially Mercury and Venus. They'll take good care of you, just like today. The stars are really interested in what will happen to you at school tomorrow, and they want to know how you're doing. They want to know if you've learned the alphabet and if you're getting along better with Rosemary."

"I don't like her," the boy said. "She kicks people and steals cookies from my lunch."

"The stars will take care of you," Jerome said softly. "When you see Rosemary, just get out of her way and do something else. She just acts funny sometimes. I know from your horoscope that you'll find plenty of crayons and clay to play with."

"A train," the boy said sleepily.

"You will find a train," Jerome said, blowing out cigar
smoke, "and you can play with the train if you share it.
Rosemary won't bother you. Anyhow, it'll be a fine day.
The planets and the stars have decided that it'll be sunny
tomorrow morning, and you'll also be playing outside in
the sandbox or the jungle gym. You'll laugh a lot and there's
a good chance you'll play hide-and-seek. I have a feeling
that there'll be peanut butter sandwiches in your lunchbox
tomorrow. Now go to sleep. Sleep tight." Half asleep, the
boy made roaring-dragon sounds. Jerome leaned back in
the rocking chair to finish his cigar and listen to Glenn Miller.

Jerome is Gregory's uncle, in actual fact. Jerome's brother
Cecil, Gregory's father, and Cecil's wife, Virginia, were on
their way back from seeing *E. T.* when they were hit head-
on in a residential area of Ann Arbor by a kid who was
testing the potential of his father's Corvette. At the time,
Jerome was living with a red-haired woman named Leslie
who was about to move out anyway: her company had re-
located her in Seattle. Very little of what happened to Jerome in this period of his life entered his permanent memory. The phone rang all the time, and he had to talk to
lawyers whose names he could never remember. He had to
go to the Hall of Justice by himself and sign documents.
Cecil and Virginia's will said quite explicitly that Jerome
was to be the guardian of Gregory should anything happen to them; Jerome had known about this will but had
thought it would never be unlocked from the safety de-
posit box where it had been stored against the day.

He took a leave from the bank and stayed with his mother
in Grosse Pointe Shores for two weeks, where he tried to
get used to the shock of his brother and sister-in-law's deaths
and to having Gregory around all the time. Jerome was
terrified of every minute of his entire future earthly life.
For his part, Gregory went back to sucking his thumb and
sat slumped in front of the television set all day, crying in
the evening when the children's programming ended. At
times he fell asleep during "Mr. Rogers' Neighborhood"
and emitted tiny snores. After Jerome had finally taken all
of his nephew's toys over to his condominium in Ann Ar-

bor, he moved Gregory out of his mother's home and into his. Six months later Jerome's mother sold her house and moved to Arizona, obviously dazed but not yet incompetent.

After a few weeks, Gregory stopped asking when his mommy and daddy were coming back, but he became more interested in television than ever, especially cartoons and broadcasts of church services. He explained to Jerome that people prayed on television, and he wanted to know how it was done. This request was the first one he had made to Jerome that did not have to do with getting dressed, going to the bathroom, or eating a meal. Jerome hadn't been brought up in a religious household, didn't know anything about prayers, and said so.

"I want to know how," Gregory said. "They all do it on TV. What do I do?"

"I don't know," Jerome told him. "But try this: kneel beside the bed at night and put your head down and close your eyes. Think of what you're happy about. Then think about the things you want. That's what people usually do when they pray." He stopped and waited. Then he asked, "Why do you want to start doing something like this?"

"It might help," Gregory said.

In this way, Jerome hit on the idea of astrology and horoscopes. He had noticed, at a time when he thought they had nothing in common, that Gregory's birthday and his own were both in May, making them Taureans. One night, while Gregory was curled at his end of the sofa watching television and he himself was reading the paper, he found Jeane Dixon's astrology column and read the entry for Taureans aloud: "Show greater confidence in yourself and others will pay more attention to your ideas and comments. You cannot handle a project all alone. Share the work—and the glory." At first Gregory said nothing, as if he hadn't heard, but then he turned to Jerome and asked, "What's that?"

Jerome explained that it was his fortune for tomorrow, and that the woman who wrote it was a kind of fortune-teller, and people believed that she could see into the fu-

ture and tell what was about to happen before it actually
happened.

"How?" Gregory asked. "How does she know?"

"It's called astrology," Jerome said. "It's based on the stars
and the planets. People think the planets have mysterious
forces. They cause things. This says you should share your
games at school tomorrow and be nice and not hog everything and not be afraid. Mostly it says not to be afraid."

"I'm not afraid," Gregory said, his eyes on the television.

"I know you're not. But here it says that the stars will
help you out not being afraid."

"Okay," Gregory said.

In Ann Arbor, a bookish town, Jerome had no trouble
finding a paperback guide to astrology. The one he chose
had a bloated, menacing star on the cover, either a red giant
or an arcane symbol of some sort. At the cash register he
felt quite sheepish, as if he had emotional difficulties that
he was trying to cure by himself, but the clerk didn't seem
to care very much about what books he bought. He took
the book to his car, drove to the nursery school, picked up
Gregory, and went home. That night, after Gregory was
asleep, he read the book straight through, dismayed by its
complexity. Casting Gregory's horoscope would take some
time. He took fifteen minutes off from his lunch break at
the bank the next day to read relevant sections of the book,
which he had brought along in his briefcase, and the next
night he began to put Gregory's horoscope together at the
kitchen table.

Sun in Taurus: constructive, practical, down-to-earth.
Jerome marked down Gregory's Earth sign, appropriate for
farmers and others with persistence and domestic virtues.
Hitler, the book informed him, had been a Taurus, as was
Walt Whitman. Discouraged, he read on. At birth, Gregory's moon was in Cancer: "You may have a strong bond
with your mother. You are good at camouflage. You excel
at impersonations." Ascendant or rising sign: Gemini.
"Gemini ascending has special problems with bankers and
clergymen." Jerome read this sentence again. "*Gemini ascending has special problems with bankers and clergymen.*" He

continued on. "You may hold several jobs at one time. You may well be divorced. You may lose your children." Jerome could not get Gregory's sign for Mercury; the procedure was too complicated. He paged through the book for Gregory's Venus sign, which was also Gemini. "Venus in Gemini makes you pleasant, sociable, and relaxed." The rest of the description applied only to adults. As for Mars, at Gregory's birth, it had been in Leo: "You are friendly. But you tend to be self-centered and see most events in your own terms. You may have a habit of blowing small things out of proportion."

"What's that?" A voice out of nowhere came from behind Jerome. He turned around and saw Mrs. Schultz looking over his shoulder at the horoscope he was constructing. She was carrying a pair of garden clippers, their blades caked with dirt.

"Mrs. Schultz! This is a horoscope. How did you get in?"

"I was tending to things. I thought this was *my* house. Your front door was unlocked, and so I came in. I get confused in this place because all these damn-fool buildings look alike." She gazed down at the table with an expression of pained amusement. "A horoscope? I thought you were a grown-up."

"I *am* a grown-up. I'm using it for Gregory. He needs it."

The noise Mrs. Schultz made could have been throat-clearing, laughter, or a cough. Jerome decided that he would not ask which one it was. "In that case," she said, "I won't stay. I'm going home, and you don't have to help me this time. I'll find my way by myself, *without* a horoscope. What's that music I hear? Glenn Miller. Well, *that* puts me back into the bloom of youth." She did not shuffle out but picked up her feet ostentatiously. Jerome watched her disappear down the hall and go out the front door, which she left open. He went back to work.

Jerome's composite horoscope for Gregory presented his nephew as a rather shaky and split character with extraordinary requirements for domestic stability. The planetary signs, however, were somewhat obtuse when they were not contradictory, so Jerome decided to change them, to revise the sky. Where there was weakness, Jerome inserted strength. Where he found indecision or calamity, he substituted resolve and good fortune. In place of trauma and loss he wrote down words like *luck* and *intelligence*. This, he thought at first, would invalidate the horoscope, but then he decided that if the planets had real influence, then they were influencing him now to alter Gregory's life-plan. It was their wish.

He put up Gregory's planetary wheel on the refrigerator door. Above the wheel he wrote down Gregory's virtue-words in blue and yellow crayon. For the next week, he explained the chart to Gregory and told him what the planets said he would be like. He explained what all the words were and what they meant. At first Gregory was silent about all this, but one morning he asked Jerome if he could take his horoscope to school. Given permission, he put the chart in his Lone Ranger lunchbox. That afternoon, when he got into the car, he said that most of the other kids wanted Jerome to make up *their* horoscopes but that the only one he really had to do was Magda Brodsky's.

"Who's Magda Brodsky?" Jerome asked.

"Somebody," Gregory said. "She's in the class."

"Is she your friend?"

"I guess so."

"What does she look like?"

"She's nice."

"I mean, what does she *look* like?"

"I told you. She's nice."

"Is she your friend?"

"I guess. She doesn't say a whole lot."

"When's her birthday?"

"I asked her. She said the fourth of July."

"Is she as old as you are?"

"Yeah."

This time, Jerome did not consult the book, although he pretended to do so whenever Gregory was in the room. He drew the wheel, wrote out the symbols for the signs in the quadrants, and then wrote down Magda Brodsky's virtues in green and orange crayon. It was like making up a calendar that had no relation to real dates or days of the week. Jerome decided that Magda was courageous, businesslike, and articulate. In addition, she was affectionate, physically agile, sensible, and generous. The adjectives came to him easily. Jerome drew a picture of Saturn at the top of the chart, along with several five-pointed stars. He told Gregory to give the chart to Magda, and he explained what all the words were, and what they meant. Gregory took the chart to school the next day.

In the evening, after dinner, Magda's mother called him. Being the assistant manager of a branch bank, Jerome had expected this call and thought he knew how to handle it.

"Hello, Mr. Birmingham? this is Amelia Brodsky." She had a pleasant but resolute voice. "Look, I don't want to disturb you, but Magda brought this sheet of paper home from school today, which she says she got from your boy. I want you to understand that I'm not objecting to it. In fact, it's made a distinct difference in her behavior this afternoon. She's been quite an angel. I just want to know what this thing is. Did you do it? Can you explain it to me?"

"I thought you'd be calling," Jerome said. "Actually, it's her horoscope, but it's not accurate. By that I mean that I made up a horoscope to give my boy some confidence, and he took it to school. When he came home he said his friend Magda wanted one, so I made up that one for her."

"Oh." Mrs. Brodsky sounded discreetly taken aback. "You see," she began, then stopped. She tried again. "You see, it's not that I think this little game is doing any harm." She paused. "What do you mean when you say it's not accurate?"

Jerome smiled and waited a moment. Then he said, "I just drew some symbols on the horoscope and listed a few virtues at the top. It's not accurate because I didn't check an ephemeris, where her planetary signs would be listed. I just wrote down some virtues I thought she might like to have. I've never met your daughter. My boy asked me to do it as a favor to her. Do you mind?"

"Well, no. That is, I don't think so. I'm not sure. I'm not a believer in astrology. Not at all. It's against my discipline.

I'm a professional biologist." She said this last sentence as if it were an astounding revelation, with pauses between the words.

"Well," Jerome said, "I don't believe in it either, and I'm a banker."

"If you don't believe in it," she asked, "why did you do it?"

Jerome had had a drink in preparation for this call, which was probably why he said, "I'm trying to learn how to be a parent."

This statement proved to be too much for Mrs. Brodsky, who rapidly thanked Jerome for explaining the whole matter to her before she hung up.

Later in the week, sitting in the dark of Gregory's room, with a cigar in his hand and Glenn Miller playing "Chattanooga Choo-Choo" softly beside him, Jerome began a bunny story. "Once upon a time, there was a bunny who lived with his mommy and daddy bunny in the bunny hole at the edge of the great green wood." All the bunny stories started with that sentence. After it, Jerome was deep in the terror of fictional improvisation. "One day the little bunny went hopping out on the bunny path in the woods when he met his friend the porcupine. The wind was blowing like this." Jerome made a wind sound, and the cigar smoke blew out of his mouth. "Together the bunny and the porcupine walked down the path, gazing at the branches that waved back and forth, when suddenly the little bunny fell into a hole. It was a deep hole that the little bunny hadn't seen, because he had been staring at the branches waving in the wind. 'Help!' he cried. 'Help!'"

"Uncle Jerome," Gregory said.

"What?"

"I don't want to hear any more bunny stories."

"Any of them? Or just this one?"

"Any of them." He brought his stuffed dragon closer to his face. "Tell me my horoscope."

"It will be warm tomorrow," Jerome said, having seen the weather reports. "It will be a fine spring day. Soon it will

be summer, and you'll be playing outside." Jerome stopped.
"You will learn to swim, and you'll take boat rides."
   Gregory's eyes opened. "I want a boat ride."
   "When?"
   "Right away."
   "What kind of boat?"
   "I don't care. I want a boat ride. Can Magda come?"
   "You want a ride in a rowboat?"
   "Sure. Can Magda come?"
   "Next Saturday," Jerome said, "if the weather is good.
You'll have to remember to invite her."
   "Don't worry," Gregory said.

   Amelia Brodsky delivered Magda promptly at nine o'clock
in the morning ten days later. She kept the pleasantries to
a minimum. She couldn't stay to chat, she said, because
she was on her way to the farmers' market, where she would
have to battle the crowds. She asked which lake they were
going to, and when Jerome said Cloverleaf Lake, Mrs.
Brodsky nodded and said there *was* a rowboat concession
there, with life jackets, and with that she kissed Magda
goodbye and left in her station wagon. Jerome had been
glad to see her go: she was well over six feet tall and wore
a button on her blouse with some slogan on it that he had
been unable to read.
   Magda was looking at him suspiciously. She was a small
girl, even for her age, with tightly curled hair and intelli-
gently watchful brown eyes. She was wearing jeans and a
pink sweatshirt that said "Say good things about Detroit"
on it, the words printed underneath a rainbow. She and
Gregory climbed into the back seat, whispering to each other
but then falling silent. Jerome looked in at them. "Do we
have everything?" he asked, feeling shaky himself. "Jackets, caps, snack, and shoes?" From his list he realized how
nervous he was. "Anybody have to go to the bathroom before we leave?" They both shook their heads. "All right,"
he said. "Here goes." He backed the car out of the driveway into the street, where Mrs. Schultz happened to be
standing, a slightly more vacant expression on her face than
was usual for her.

"Where are you going?" she asked, through the open
window on the driver's side.

"Boating," Jerome said.

Mrs. Schultz's right hand flew to the door handle,
clutching it. "Take me along," she said.

"Take her along." It was Gregory. Jerome turned around
and stared at him.

"Mrs. Schultz? You want Mrs. Schultz along with us on
our boat ride?" Both Gregory and Magda nodded together.

"I don't get this," Jerome said aloud, before turning to Mrs.
Schultz. "I suppose if you want to come along, you can.
Are you dressed for it? Is your house locked up?"

"Doesn't matter." She walked around to the passenger
side and got into the front seat, slamming the door fiercely.
"Let them steal everything, for all I care. I want to go out
in a boat. Let's get going."

On the ten-minute drive to the lake, Magda kept silent,
though she would nod if either Jerome or Gregory asked
her a question. Meanwhile, in the front seat, Mrs. Schultz
was watching the landscape with her eyes wide open, as if
she had never ridden in an automobile before. She was
offering opinions. "I'm glad it's Saturday," she said. "If this
was during the week, I'd be missing 'Days of Our Lives.'"
They passed a water tower. "Never saw one of those before." Jerome groaned. Mrs. Schultz suddenly turned her
gaze on Jerome and asked him, "What does the horoscope
say about today, Jerome?"

"It'll be beautiful. It *is* beautiful. Warm. Nothing to worry
about."

"No episodes?"

"No. Definitely no episodes."

"Good." She drew in a deep breath. "I'm too old for episodes."

When they reached the lake, Jerome paid to get into the
grounds of the state park, which included a beach and
boating area. The two children and the old woman did not
seem especially pleased about arriving; nobody announced it. They all stepped out of the car in silence as the
moist vegetative smell of the lake drifted up to them. "Any-

body have to go to the bathroom?" Jerome asked again, being careful to take the snack bag from the back seat. They all shook their heads. "Well, in that case, let's go," he said, and they walked down to the rowboat concession, Mrs. Schultz leading, while Gregory held on to Jerome's hand and Magda held on to Gregory's.

The boy in the concession stand, who was listening to a transistor radio and wearing a Styx T-shirt, tied them all into life jackets, Mrs. Schultz, because of her arthritis, being the hardest to fit. This job finished, he went down to the dock and pulled an aluminum rowboat out to where some steps had been built in the dock's north side. Magda and Gregory went in front, Mrs. Schultz in back, and Jerome sat down in the middle, where he could row. "You got an hour," the boy said, scratching his chest. "If you take longer, it's okay, but you got to pay extra when you get back." Jerome nodded as he lifted the oars. "You know how to row?"

"I know how," Jerome said. "Cast us off." The boy untied the boat and gave it a push.

"Bon voyage," he said, lifting his leg to scratch his ankle.

Jerome watched the dock recede. Mrs. Schultz was observing something in the distance and sniffing the air. Both Magda and Gregory were staring down into the water. "How far do we go?" Jerome asked them all.

"To the middle," Gregory said. "I want to go to the middle."

"Yes, that would be fine," Mrs. Schultz said. "Right to the middle."

"Okay." He felt a slight ache in his shoulders. "If anybody wants a snack," he said, "there are crackers and things in that bag." He stopped rowing with his right hand to point to the bag, and, as he did, the boat turned in the water.

"Come on," Gregory said. "Don't do that. Just row."

"Be nice," Mrs. Schultz said to Gregory. "Always try to be nice."

Like most lakes in the southern part of the state, Cloverleaf was rather shallow and no more than six miles in circumference. All the houses on the shore, most of them summer cabins, were distinctly visible. A slight breeze from the west blew over them. With the sky blue, and the temperature in the low seventies, Jerome, as he rowed, felt his heart loosen in his chest while the mildness of the day crept over him. He could see several families splashing in the water at the public beach. He smiled, and noticed that Mrs. Schultz was doing the same.

"Tell me when we get to the middle of the lake," Jerome said. "Somebody tell me when we're there."

"I'll tell you," Magda said. It was her first complete public sentence of the day.

"Thank you, Magda," Jerome said, turning around to see her. She was doing finger-flicks in the water.

Five minutes later she broke the silence by saying, "We're there." Jerome raised the oars from the water and let the droplets fall one by one before he brought them into the boat. On the south side of the lake an outboard was pulling a waterskier wearing a blue safety vest. Gregory was letting his hand play in the water, humming a song from the Glenn Miller tape, and Magda was now staring down into the water with her nose only four inches or so from its surface. "I see a monster down there," she said. No one seemed surprised. "It's got a long neck and an ugly head."

"A reptile," Mrs. Schultz said, nodding. "Like Loch Ness."

"It could bite," Gregory said, "Watch out."

"Sea monsters," Jerome said, "may not be extinct. Pass me the crackers, please."

"After I have mine," Mrs. Schultz said, her hand in the bag. She was sniffing the air again. "I don't believe I have ever seen a sea monster, not this far inland. I've heard about them, though." She waited. "I like this lake. It's a nice lake."

"There's a bug on me," Magda said, tapping a finger on her sweatshirt. "There. It flew away."

"Pass me a cracker," Gregory said. "Please."

"Look at that waterskier," Jerome said. "He's very good."

The rowboat began to drift, pushed by the breeze. Gregory munched on his cracker, and now Magda was dipping her fingers in the water and experimenting with wave motion. Mrs. Schultz had taken a handkerchief out of her sleeve and put it on her head, apparently to minimize the danger of sunstroke.

"Does anybody want anything?" Jerome asked, feeling regal.

"No," the other three said.

"Don't ask me if I have to go to the bathroom," Mrs. Schultz complained. "Once is enough." She waited. "Do you know," she said, "that my grandfather owned land just north of here? He was Scottish, and, of all things, his life's dream was to build himself a golf course. He was even going to build the hills. But, for some reason, it didn't happen. Instead, he learned how to play the oboe and could play it lying down in a hammock, during the summer. He had the lungs of a seven-year-old boy." She looked at Jerome. "He never smoked cigars."

"What's that?" Magda asked. Her finger was pointing toward shore.

"What's what?"

"That." She was still pointing. "That smoke."

"That's a charcoal grill," Jerome said. "Somebody's cooking hamburgers outside, and that's where all the smoke comes from."

"Cooking with charcoal is bad for you," Mrs. Schultz said. "Too much carbon. Cancer."

"Where's the grill?" Magda asked. "I don't see it."

They all turned to look. Thin strips of smoke rose in the distance behind or near a house. It was hard to tell. The house was a plain white one that seemed to have a screen porch but no other distinguishing features.

"Is that house on fire?" Magda asked.

"No," Jerome said. "It is *not* on fire. *They are just cooking hamburgers.*" He did not want to shout. "It's Saturday. People cook hamburgers on Saturday all the time." Because there was more smoke, he felt he should raise his voice somewhat. "You shouldn't worry."

"Maybe we ought to row toward it," Mrs. Schultz suggested, the handkerchief on her head fluttering somewhat as her head shook.

"No," Jerome said. "I don't think so. The children should stay away."

"Look," Gregory said, "they're so small."

"Is there someone inside the house?" Magda asked, and

began to cry. "I hope there isn't anyone inside. What if there's someone inside the house?"

"It's not a fire!" Jerome shouted, unable to stop himself. "They're just cooking lunch! You'd see flames if it was a fire!"

While they stared, the boat rocked gently underneath them. A fish jumped behind them and slapped the water. The breeze brought them a scent of smoke. Jerome turned around and glanced at the opposite side of the lake, where the boy in the rowboat concession was sitting with his feet up in the booth. Gregory reached out for Jerome's hand. "You didn't know about this yesterday," Gregory said. "It wasn't in the horoscope. Daddy, Magda's crying."

"I know," Jerome said. "She'll be all right."

"I want to know if someone's in the house," Magda said. Mrs. Schultz was murmuring and muttering. "I want to know," Magda repeated.

Suddenly Mrs. Schultz stared at Jerome. "You said there wouldn't be any episodes," she said, pointing her finger at him. "God damn it, you said nothing would happen to us! And look at what's happening!" She was shouting, "Look at all the smoke and the fire!" Her finger, still pointing, pointed now at Jerome, Magda, and Gregory.

"Mrs. Schultz," Jerome begged, "please don't swear. There are children here."

"It's a fire," she repeated. And then she turned around in the boat, bent down, and cupped her hands in the water. Raising her arms, she doused her head. The water streamed into her gray hair and washed the handkerchief off, so that it dropped onto the gunwales of the rowboat. Again she reached down into the lake and again she scooped a small quantity of water over her head. As the children and Jerome watched, handful by handful the old woman soaked her hair, her skin, and her clothes, as if she were making a formal gesture toward the accidents of life, which in their monotonous regularity had brought her to her present condition.

Weights

When Tobias slipped open his usual locker, he saw someone else's white sock inside, soaking wet. It smelled of sweat, or of living matter washed up by the ocean. Instead of picking it up and putting it on the floor, he moved down to the next locker, number fifty-eight. The Y didn't assign lockers, but Tobias thought of number fifty-six as his, territorially. It had been the year of his birth and was no trouble to remember, even when he was blasted after a workout. A month after he had started his program he had blanked on his locker number and had had to sit for ten minutes straight before he could think of it, his sweat cooling in layers on his skin and clothes. After that he went to a number planted in his unconscious: his birth year, his parents' street address.

He stripped off his street clothes in the usual order: shoes, socks, pants, shirt, watch, underwear. He stood naked, breathing steadily, feeling his heart accelerate, then reached down into his gym bag for the jock, sweat suit, socks, weight belt, shoes, and gloves. At the bottom of the bag was a copy of *The Maltese Falcon* for the bus ride home. He scowled at the book and crammed the gym bag into the locker, his hands getting damp as he heard the clank of plates falling on each other.

Brian, a young laid-off cop, was doing bench presses on the Universal machine, grunting and arching his back. Tobias went over to spot for him. Brian's thick arms were trembling, and his forehead underneath his curly hair was plum-colored.

"Easy," Tobias said softly. "Easy up you got it there Brian come on be proud do it one more finish it all right come on all right." Brian yowled, brought the bar down with a chrome-on-chrome crash, and Tobias clasped his hand and pulled him up. They didn't say anything at first; then Brian said, "Shit," and walked over to the water fountain. Tobias went to the opposite side of the room for warm-ups. After

a minute, he stepped over to the bench where Brian had
been and increased the weights.

Tobias had started to take an interest in his health after
he had been laid off for the third time. He had taught history in a high school before enrollments declined and he
was released. He found a job as a bartender at a chrome-
and-molded-plastic restaurant in Ann Arbor where young
singles met for quiche and salad. When the recession cut
into disposable income, Tobias was pink-slipped. Using
willpower against panic, he found a job as a night clerk at
a Howard Johnson's. But then people seemed to stop trav-
eling. So he collected unemployment insurance and sat in
his girlfriend's apartment, eating Fritos and playing his guitar
to Carlos Montoya records. The apartment had a southern
exposure and a good view, and all through September Tobias sat in the sun, refusing to think. At five, Miriam would
come home from the hospital where she worked. By October, she had lost her smile, and Tobias knew that he would
lose his position as her lover within two weeks.

"Tobias," she said, coming in. She took off her nurse's
shoes and lit up a cigarette. "Any luck?"

"I haven't been out all day," he said, then shrugged and
smiled.

"Are you depressed?" she asked. "You seem depressed."

"I'm unemployed. That makes a difference."

She blew out a puff of smoke. "Your depression is making *me* depressed. I wish you were busy. You know: with
some kind of life."

"I've had a life," he said, putting down the guitar in a
solemn way. "I've had quite a few jobs, after all. They keep
firing me. It's not exactly my fault that I'm not working."

"You aren't persistent," she said, leaning back. "You don't
act like a success. You've got to peddle yourself. Be aggressive. You've got—" She made a vague gesture. "You've got
to show them."

"Show them what?"

"Show them how smart you are. Show them your degrees. *I* know how smart you are. You've got a lot of degrees."

"I sure do," he said, happy to agree with her about himself. "Lots of useless degrees." He held up two fingers, and they both said, "*Two* master's degrees," simultaneously, without smiling.

"So try computer programming," she suggested.

"Those people aren't getting jobs in Michigan," he said. "Not any more." He opened a new bag of Fritos. "No one's getting jobs here." He munched thoughtfully. "Nobody."

"I've got a job!" she said. "Someone has to have a job."

"You're a nurse. People are sicker than ever. You were always a nurse. People pay you to do what you do." He smiled. "It's different."

"No, it isn't. You just sit around. It's funny, but it's getting so I can't stand that."

"What's for dinner?" he interrupted, pulling his hand through his hair.

"There's nothing for dinner." Bending down, she pulled a twenty-dollar bill out of her purse. She carefully folded it into a paper airplane and flew it toward him. It nosedived in front of his guitar, and Tobias had to pick it up. "Get us some dinner, love," she said, walking toward the bathroom.

In Spanish, Tobias said, "I don't like it when you show contempt for me."

"Speak English. What did you say? God, I hate it when you do that." She closed the bathroom door.

He unfolded the bill and put it in his pocket. "I'll walk," he said. "Take your time in there."

Two hours later, he came back carrying a large brown paper bag. Miriam was asleep on the sofa and woke up when he came in. "My God," she said, "I thought you'd been robbed. Where were you? What took you so long? I'm starving."

"I can explain." He put the bag on the kitchen table and then turned to her, smiling an odd smile. "It was a nice evening. I decided to walk over to Nature's Harvest. I thought I was going to buy some eggs, but there was this salesgirl who said that what I needed was some vitamin C." He pulled out a brown plastic bottle with speckled orange pills in it. "She said that people in my condition also need magnesium and trace minerals, and I thought: why not?" He pulled out a smaller bottle whose pills were brown and oval-shaped. "And B-complex." Another bottle. "And a protein supplement, loaded with vitamins *and* trace minerals." He showed her a can with a yellow label, on which was printed a photograph of a man and a woman, both wearing swimsuits. "She said that bad nutrition was the cause of what I'm feeling. So: no more Fritos. Maybe she was cuckoo, but I thought, what the hell."

Miriam, now in her jeans, stared through the doorway into the kitchen, though she hadn't moved from the sofa. "Is that what you got us for dinner?"

"I sort of forgot about the dinner."

"Tobias, it's been *two hours*."

"Well, I enjoyed the walk."

She closed her eyes. "How soon can you be out of here? Is a week much too fast for you?"

"You want me to move out?"

"We don't like each other now, do we?"

"No," he said, examining the label on one of the bottles. "I guess not."

"Well then. Can you move out by the weekend?"

"That's pretty soon. I don't have any money. I'll have to plan."

"That's your problem," she said. "Do what you have to do. Take yourself somewhere. I've had it." Her voice was rising. "The sooner the better. No more of this. No more vitamins. No more Carlos Montoya. No more friends worrying about you."

Tobias shrugged and bent down experimentally to touch his toes.

The salesgirl at Nature's Harvest was named Gerri, and, unlike Miriam, she didn't keep many books around the apartment. Instead, her walls were decorated with posters of forests and seal puppies. Tobias had gone back to Nature's Harvest each day for the next week, and he and Gerri discovered that they had attended the same elementary school in Oak Park, a suburb of Detroit, and had had the same third-grade teacher, Miss Heseltine, four years apart. Gerri had been attending the University of Michigan but had dropped out to explore her other possibilities. Her considerable overbite gave her face an unlucky aura. She invited him over for dinner, and after dessert he explained his life situation to her. She was intrigued. Secretly his heart was pumping hard. From the shoulders up, Gerri was not beautiful and seemed rather stupid, unlike Miriam. She would never fire him as her lover. He would get her to reenroll in the university and then become essential to her by doing her homework. In time he would find some sort of serious job. It would work out. Gerri was chewing sugarless gum, and, as they talked, she would stop chewing long enough to give him a smile.

He put an ad in *The Ann Arbor News* offering to do housepainting, lawn work, and home fix-it jobs at competitive rates. His ad went into a long column of other such ads. In three weeks he received two calls. One was from a woman who wanted him to walk her Pomeranian. The other was more serious and involved his cleaning out a basement and hauling away the trash in his Volkswagen Beetle to the city dump. He earned thirty dollars for that. Instead of renewing the ad, he let it lapse. On days when Gerri didn't have to work, she would bring him along with her as she jogged. She was in excellent condition; she had displaced all her pride and vanity into her legs.

One day she ran him over to the Y and told him he should become familiar with the facilities. He went into the weight room. With all the noise and hard breathing, it reminded him of his high school locker room after a good baseball game. It was a mindless collective. He joined the Y the next day, using money he borrowed from Gerri. Andrew, the scholarly black attendant in the weight room who wore bifocals and had the physique of a linebacker, put him on a program for beginners but quickly modified it as Tobias made progress through the first three months. Tobias started coming in every day, and Andrew said he had never seen anyone make so much progress so fast. Never.

Tobias now had a third eye. This eye was in the middle
of his forehead, and when he was doing his sets the eye
would shine a beam of sharply focused particle energy toward a point. The point could be both inside and outside
of his body. He could make the energy flow toward his
hands when he was doing sets, such as preacher curls, that
required force contracted or extended in an arc. Most of the
time the beam of energy turned inward. It charged his spine
with positive electrical ions. When the eye was open, he
felt like a bomb that had been cleverly converted into a
multipurpose generator. The eye was especially tolerant of
anger. It fed on anger and knew how to channel its ten-
sions throughout the body out into the gloved hands. Tobias had never known how much like the sun his anger
was—how brilliantly it radiated.

In the morning, Tobias would stand in lines and fill out
applications that were always printed on yellow or orange
paper. On bad days, the secretaries would tell him right
away the particulars of his overqualifications. By lunch-
time Tobias's third eye was beginning to open. If it had been
sleeping, it was now alert and awake, red with unwobbling
pinwheel anger, its thermonuclear heat stoking up on his
forehead. At that moment he would pack his gym bag and
jog to the Y. By winter, the contempts visited upon him all
morning enlarged his spirit and drove him, inspired,
through the long afternoons. Andrew, approvingly, told him,
"Some people get mad and eat. They eat and they eat. You
do this."

When Gerri came home from Nature's Harvest, she liked
to make love. Because of her face, she had never had a
steady lover, and now that she did, she took advantage of
her opportunity. But in November Tobias arrived home early
and found her sitting in the living room with a man he'd
never seen before. They were both eating ice cream di-
rectly from the carton. Tobias smelled pot.
    "Hi," he said. "What a surprise."
    "Tobias." Her voice stayed flat. "I took the afternoon off.
I was sort of tired. This is Patrick."

Patrick smiled slightly, dropped his spoon into the container, and raised his hand upward and out from his face. "Pleased to meet you, Tobias," he said, his lips smeared with chocolate. Tobias shook his hand before taking his gym bag into the bedroom. Since they never made the bed, he couldn't tell if it had been used. He wasn't jealous; he was afraid Gerri would leave him. He came back to the living room.

"Where have you been today?" she asked.

"At the Y. Other places."

"Tobias," she said, turning to Patrick, "is very big on physical fitness. He could break you in two."

Patrick smiled and continued to eat ice cream. "No kidding!"

She nodded. Tobias looked at her. "You're stoned," he said.

She nodded again. "We used up *all* the dope," she admitted.

"All of it?"

"I guess we must be pigs," Patrick confessed. "Are you angry?"

"I don't know," Tobias said. "Are you old friends or something?"

Patrick nodded, but Gerri shook her head. "Well," Tobias asked, "which is it?"

"Yes and no," Patrick said. "We *might* be old friends. We met two years ago but haven't seen each other since."

Tobias was still standing. "Before today."

"Right."

Tobias stood over to the side and waited. At last he said, "Something I should know here?"

Patrick closed the lid over the ice cream and shook his head. "Nope. Nothing here at all, man." He lifted himself up from the chair and put the spoon and the ice cream carefully on the floor. "Tobias," he said, holding his hand out for a shake. Tobias shook it. "Gotta run. I'll be seeing you." Tobias nodded. "Good luck with the weights." Neither Patrick nor Gerri looked at each other as Patrick made his way toward the door.

"I hope he makes it home," Gerri said. "He's real wrecked.

And," she added, "he's a bad driver." She stopped eating.
"I suppose I should ask how this makes you feel."

"I feel like stepping on your face," he said, picking at his
fingernails.

"Don't do that," she said. "I'm too stoned. Are you going
to come at me with a knife?"

"No."

"I know how men go crazy," she said. "Are you going to
do that?"

"No."

"You aren't the sort of man who beats women up."

"That's right," he said. "I can't."

"Tobias, it wasn't anything serious. We just met at Hud-
son's and came home. Actually," and here she stood up and
raised her hand to stroke him on the side of the head, "once
we got home, he didn't attract me at all. I mean, *you* saw
him. So what are you worried about? You're beautiful." She
smiled. "Really, you are. You're gorgeous. You haven't been
insulted."

He went into the bathroom, shut the door, and sat in the
bathtub for an hour, until Gerri called for him. He was
thinking of wars: of rockets, submarines, and exploding
gasoline cannisters.

Here is what he ate: at breakfast, four eggs, two cups of
milk, an orange, a protein supplement, and six vitamin pills.
For lunch he downed yogurt with wheat germ, three ounces
of tuna, and broiled liver, along with another two cups of
milk. For dinner he consumed two servings of broiled fish,
garbanzo beans, and a salad of spinach, tomatoes, sar-
dines, anchovies, onions, cheese, and salami. He was
gaining weight from 125 grams of protein each day. Gerri,
who approved of this diet, was stealing the food from Nature's Harvest, where the procedures for checking inven-
tory had not been clarified.

Plant closings were announced almost every week. The
weight room at the Y filled up with the unemployed. Laid-
off men watched Tobias, concealing their amazement. Then
they introduced themselves and asked for advice. These

questions broke his concentration, dragging him away from
the silent battlefield where, every hour, he imagined several bloody victories.

He had sold the Volkswagen and now walked everywhere or took the bus. In December, as he was leaving a
grocery store, a golden retriever trotted up to him and
wagged his tail. The dog had an intelligent, quizzical face,
with a long sleek forehead: a university dog. Tobias bent
down and patted him. The dog's mouth opened, and he
panted with affection, his breath visible in the cold air. When
Tobias started walking, the dog followed him.

When he arrived home, he went out into the backyard.
Standing under a dwarf apple tree, he told the dog to sit.
The dog sat. Tobias walked over to the other side of the
yard. "Come here, Andy," he said. The dog remained seated.
"Come here, Archy. Come here, Ace. Come here Alfie." He
went through all the A names he knew and was in the
middle of the B's and had said, "Come here, Boris," when
the dog stood up, boot-camp style, and ran over
to him.

"So your name is Boris, huh?" The dog wagged his tail
in agreement. Tobias felt around the dog's neck for a collar
or nametag but found nothing. "Are you hungry?" He
brought him inside and broiled some hamburger from Gerri's side of the refrigerator.

When she came home, Tobias and Boris were sleeping
on the bed next to each other, the dog's paws over Tobias's
chest. The dog woke up and barked as she came into the
room, but Tobias told him to shut up, and he did. "This is
Boris," Tobias said. Gerri smiled. She lay down next to Tobias and kissed him. They pushed the dog off the bed as
they made love, which for the first time reminded Tobias
of some obscure form of exercise.

When they were finished, Gerri looked down at Tobias.
"You should see yourself. My God." But he knew what he
looked like and his eyes were closed.

On her days off, Gerri said she wanted to laze around
the apartment with Tobias. The first two times she made

this request, he agreed, but when she asked again, on a Thursday, he said no.

"Why not?"

"I have to go to the Y."

"You were there yesterday."

"I was there yesterday, and I'll be there tomorrow. I have to go today."

"For how long?"

"I don't know. Two hours minimum."

"Take a day off."

"There are *no* days off. If I stop, I'll spoil it, and I can't stop."

"Why not?"

"It's pulling me. It's impossible to explain."

"So why are you doing it?"

"I'm in training."

"For what?"

"I don't know."

"Let's lie around in bed all day."

"No," he said.

"Let's lie in bed," she repeated slowly, "and do anything we want to do to each other. Then let's fall asleep and do it again." They were in the kitchen, standing, and she was drinking orange juice and giving him a steady look. "I love you and that's all I want. I want to make love, and I want to do it with you." She came over to him, put her arms around his waist, and hugged him. "Aaaahhhrrr," she groaned, "why do I always have to be the one? Give me some help."

He stood motionless. Slowly his hands came up to her shoulders, where they rested. She leaned her head into his chest. He wondered how much she weighed.

"I don't want to," he said.

Her hands dropped away, though she continued leaning against him, her arms now at her sides. "Some women," she said.

He looked down. "Some women what?"

"Huh?"

"You didn't finish your sentence."

"Yes, I did. Anybody else would know. Well." She moved

away from him. "Guess I'll go shopping. Or maybe I'll have a beer. There are some friends I want to see. I may not be back for dinner. I don't know. Don't plan on me."

"Okay."

She turned around and walked out, shaking her head.

During his workout, while doing leg extensions, he ran through some songs in his head until he settled on Roy Orbison's "Pretty Woman," which had just the right nagging insistent bass line. His endurance had improved so that he needed to rest only a minute or so between sets. After leg extensions, he did leg curls, then squats; then he started bench presses, dumbbell incline presses, and lat pulldowns on the Universal machine. There were curls, tricep extensions, and sit-ups still to be done, and by the time he got to them he had gone through "Pretty Woman," "Laugh Laugh," "96 Tears," "Brown Sugar," and "I Got a Line on You." The eye in the center of his forehead had not yet opened, so during the last half hour he looked in the mirror to center himself. Brian, the unemployed cop, came over to help him. He was huffing. With his short curly hair, blue cop's eyes gone slightly wild, and thick arms, he scared newcomers, who also noticed Brian's creosotelike smell.

"Come on," Brian said, "do it. No pain, no gain."

Tobias struggled to finish, imagining how much he hated cops. "Man," he said when he was through, "I always figure you're going to arrest me if I don't do the set. Take me away in the patrol car."

"Don't I wish," Brian said. "Don't I just wish. These days, a person can get away with any damn thing he wants to, like that sloppy set you just did. It's a shame. I tell you, buddy, there's nobody out there to arrest *any*body anymore. They've all been sacked. The animals are taking over the jungle." He turned around, stretched, and put his left hand on his right arm, tensed the muscle, and nodded to himself. "I could tell you stories. I know what people are getting away with. I think about it a lot." He looked at Tobias carefully. "*I* think about it. I mean, I know how to break-and-enter. I know about those alarm systems. Why don't I do it? I don't because I'm not there yet. But I lie awake nights." Tobias nodded. They were both panting softly. "When my old lady wakes up, she looks at me, and then she goes back to sleep. She knows what I'm thinking, but she doesn't say anything, because she knows what it'll get her if she says it. She knows her place. And she knows I'm out there on the streets, in my mind, on the prowl. But you," and here he put a hand for a moment on Tobias's elbow, "you work out here like you already *did* the crime. So tell me, man, what are you running from?"

"Nothing."

"Save the bullshit for the dinnertable. You can tell your friend Brian. I mean, shit, you have put on thirty-five pounds solid of body weight since you started coming here. The amateurs are watching you, my friend, and wondering where you get it from. You come down here and you get down humming rock-and-roll instead of groaning like these other assholes. And I have discovered your secret. I am telling you that I have. All I want to know is the particulars. It's guilt, right? What'd you do?"

"I haven't done it yet."

"Did you lay a hand on your woman?"

"Gerri? No, I'm not into that."

"What about the other one? The one you told me about. Big Nurse."

"No."

"So what'd you do? You don't steal. You don't set fires. You are an educated type. I've seen those books in your gym bag. So tell me, man, what do you do?"

"Lay off, Brian. This isn't the station house."

"It's the station house, if I'm in it. Come on, Tobias my man, everybody has his crime. There was never a time without crime. What's yours?"

Tobias exhaled, smiled, turned to Brian and said, "I kill dogs."

"You do what?"

Tobias said, slowly enough for Brian to catch all of it, "I've got a rifle. I go out in my car on weekends. Sunday mornings are best. Everyone's in church. I go out where the farms are, you know, where the dogs are chained to the front yard. Sometimes there's a doghouse. I take the rifle out of the car and I shoot the dog. Sometimes in the head, sometimes in the heart. If I'm in a real bad mood I plug them in the gut. They take longer to die that way. It's the agonizing death, y'know? I've done it at night but you can't always see them, so I've been disappointed at times."

"You don't own a car. I know that. You come here on the bus."

"Okay. I don't own a car."

"I don't think you own a rifle, either. I have this feeling about you that you couldn't load a weapon if you had to."

"Brian, you are right again. I don't own a rifle."

"Yeah?" Brian scratched his hair, and drops of sweat fell from his scalp to the floor. "So do you kill dogs?"

"Not yet."

"It's pretty sick. What is it between you and dogs?"

Tobias shrugged. "It's welfare. I can't stand welfare. For anything."

"Jesus," Brian said. He turned around. "You got it worse than I do."

"So?" Tobias said to his back. "So?"

After he turned the key in the lock, he heard Boris's barking. The retriever jumped up so that his paws were on Tobias's chest; he licked him on the face. Tobias gave him some dried dogfood, then poured him some fresh water. It was dark outside, and the streets were slippery. It might be easy to get a car to run over the dog. "You want to go for a walk?" Boris wagged his tail.

He had his hand on the doorknob when the phone rang. It was Gerri, who sounded drunk. She was in a bar and told Tobias to come down right away. In the background was the blare of loud music. Her voice sounded strange, so Tobias agreed.

The bar had a large dance floor with a particle-mirror ball overhead. When Tobias arrived, Gerri was bent over her table as if examining it for flaws. Tobias surveyed the place for friends but saw no one he knew. He touched Gerri's hand. She gazed up slowly, her mouth open. "I wanted to dance," she said. "I wanted you to come here because I wanted to dance and for you to see me."

"All right," Tobias said. "Let's do that."

She took his hand and led him out. The song's rhythms were early sixties, fast, prewar. Gerri moved as if she had been living inside the song for twenty years, witty and sexual moves. Tobias tried to find a beat that would accept him, but each time he thought he had found it, the song pushed him back out. His body jerked against the startled and unsteady air, but all his movements were slow, timed for dead lifts. He felt stranded inside the arc of his body, his musculature. Then he saw Gerri looking at him. She was laughing.

"Tobias," she said. "You dance like a psychotic."

The eye in his forehead looked down at her, and he reached forward around her waist and pulled her to him. He stopped her virtuoso dancing by holding her, by making her feel the accomplishment of his back.

"Take me home," she said. "I want to mess around."

Two hours later Tobias rose from the bed and went to the bathroom. He turned on the light and looked at himself a long time in the mirror. He clicked off the light and went into the bedroom, where he dressed in the dark.

He walked to the hall, put on his overcoat, and called the dog. Boris padded over to him and they went out together.

Late March: a light snow. Tobias jogged down the sidewalk, the dog near him, patiently calm. For two blocks he watched the cars, waiting for an old one with bad brakes, while Boris peed on a lightpole. At the right moment, Tobias jumped out into the street, and Boris followed. Tobias stopped, lost his balance on the ice, then leaped backward. The dog stopped, skidded, moved back. But the car, a '68 rust-speckled Camaro, swerved, went into a spin, and struck a blue Chevette parked in the street. Something like a cloud puffed up from the Camaro's engine, and Tobias saw a spider web bloom inside the glass on the driver's side. Green liquid, radiator fluid, dribbled down into the snow. Boris sat down on the sidewalk. Meanwhile, Tobias ran to the car, where a teenager with a drunk look on his face stared in shock from behind the wheel, blood oozing in parallel lines from his forehead, already scarred from some other accident. Beside him on the driveshaft hump was an emptied six-pack, its bottles scattered over the floor. On the passenger side a woman wearing a cap with a visor was groaning, sounding like someone in childbirth. Bent forward as if kissing the dashboard, she looked peculiar, with her left arm raised in an improbable position. A splash of blood discolored the ashtray and the radio dial.

"You'll be all right," Tobias shouted. "You'll be okay."

The driver reached down a bloody hand for the latch, all the time staring at Tobias. The door would only open part of the way, and Tobias did not pull at it. Wavering, pushing his legs through the opening, the teenager eased out of the car, fell to his knees in the snow, then stood up.

"You jumped in front of me," he said tonelessly. "I was tryin' to evade you." Inside, his girlfriend was still groaning.

"I wanted you to hit my dog," Tobias said softly.

Tobias felt something on the side of his head. He felt it again. Then he realized that the teenager was attempting to hit him. Specks of blood from his forehead were falling into the snow. The boy's fists were like seeds in a windstorm: tiny, stinging without impact.

"You wrecked my car," the boy shouted. "I worked hard for this car."

The boy lay out in the snow after Tobias hit him. Some bystander grabbed Tobias's elbow, and Tobias hit him, too. Six months of continual weight training gave Tobias enough strength to deck another man who was interfering: it required only one blow. The faces moved back. Boris was barking. Tobias held his fists up into the air and noticed that at night snow looks more gray than white. The moon was a smile without a face, pasted into the winter sky. He felt like hitting someone else, but no one was against him.

He ran back to the apartment. People shouted after him. Inside, he undressed in the hallway and got into bed.

"Tobias."

"Yes."

"Where were you?"

"Boris wanted to go out. But then I lost him." He was panting. "I looked all over. I called for him."

"He'll be all right." She sniffed. "What do you smell of? You smell funny."

"Snow," he said.

"Snow doesn't smell," she said. "It's more like blood."

To silence her, he put his lips over hers and thrust his tongue into her mouth. He moved his body in the bed so that all his weight was above her, and he parted her legs and quickly entered her. Under his tongue he could tell she was making some sort of sound. He didn't enjoy kissing her, but it excited him, and so he went on doing it as her hands reached for his hair.

Harmony of the World

In the small Ohio town where I grew up, many homes had parlors that contained pianos, sideboards, and sofas, heavy objects signifying gentility. These pianos were rarely tuned. They went flat in summer around the Fourth of July and sharp in winter at Christmas. Ours was a Story and Clark. On its music stand were copies of Stephen Foster and Ethelbert Nevin favorites, along with one Chopin prelude that my mother would practice for twenty minutes every three years. She had no patience, but since she thought Ohio—all of it, every scrap—made sense, she was happy and did not need to practice anything. Happiness is not infectious, but somehow her happiness infected my father, a pharmacist, and then spread through the rest of the household. My whole family was obstinately cheerful. I think of my two sisters, my brother, and my parents as having artificial, pasted-on smiles, like circus clowns. They apparently thought cheer and good Christian words were universals, respected everywhere. The pianos were part of this cheer. They played for celebrations and moments of pleasant pain. Or rather, someone played them, but not too well, since excellent playing would have been faintly antisocial. "Chopin," my mother said, shaking her head as she stumbled through the prelude. "Why is he famous?"

When I was six, I received my first standing ovation. On the stage of the community auditorium, where the temperature was about ninety-four degrees, sweat fell from my forehead onto the piano keys, making their ivory surfaces slippery. At the conclusion of the piece, when everyone stood up to applaud, I thought they were just being nice. My playing had been mediocre; only my sweating had been extraordinary. Two years later, they stood up again. When I was eleven, they cheered. By that time I was astonishing these small-town audiences with Chopin and Rachmaninoff recital chestnuts. I thought I was a genius and read biographies of Einstein. Already the townspeople were saying that I was the best thing Parkersville had ever seen, *that I would put the place on the map.* Mothers would send their children by to watch me practice. The kids sat with their mouths open while I polished off more classics.

Like many musicians, I cannot remember ever playing badly, in the sense of not knowing what I was doing. In high school, my identity was being sealed shut: my classmates called me "el señor longhair," even though I wore a crewcut, this being the 1950s. Whenever the town needed a demonstration of local genius, it called upon me. There were newspaper articles detailing my accomplishments, and I must have heard the phrase *future concert career* at least two hundred times. My parents smiled and smiled as I collected applause. My senior year I gave a solo recital and was hired for umpteen weddings and funerals. I was good luck. On the Fourth of July the townspeople brought a piano out to the city square so that I could improvise music between explosions at the fireworks display. Just before I left for college, I noticed that our neighbors wanted to come up to me, ostensibly for small talk, but actually to touch me.

In college I made a shocking discovery: other people existed in the world who were as talented as I was. If I sat down to play a Debussy etude, they would sit down and play Beethoven, only faster and louder than I had. I felt their breath on my neck. Apparently there were other small towns. In each one of these small towns there was a genius. Perhaps some geniuses were not actually geniuses. I practiced constantly and began to specialize in the non-Germanic piano repertoire. I kept my eye out for students younger than I was, who might have flashier technique. At my senior recital I played Mozart, Chopin, Ravel, and Debussy, with encore pieces by Scriabin and Thomson. I managed to get the audience to stand up for the last time.

I was accepted into a large midwestern music school, famous for its high standards. Once there, I discovered that genius, to say nothing of talent, was a common commodity. Since I was only a middling composer, with no interesting musical ideas as such, I would have to make my career as a performer or teacher. But I didn't want to teach, and as a performer I lacked pizzazz. For the first time, it occurred to me that my life might be evolving into something unpleasant, something with the taste of stale bread.

I was beginning to meet performers with more confidence than I had, young musicians to whom doubt was as alien as proper etiquette. Often these people dressed like tramps, smelled, smoked constantly, were gay or sadistic. Whatever their imbalances, they were not genteel. *They did not represent small towns.* I was struck by their eyes. Their eyes seemed to proclaim, "The universe believes in me. It always has."

My piano teacher was a man I will call Luther Stecker. Every year he taught at the music school for six months. For the following six months he toured. He turned me away from the repertoire with which I was familiar and demanded that I learn several pieces by composers whom I had not often played, including Bach, Brahms, and Liszt. Each one of these composers discovered a weak point in me: I had trouble keeping up the consistent frenzy required by Liszt, the mathematical precision required by Bach, the unpianistic fingerings of Brahms.

I saw Stecker every week. While I played, he would doze off. When he woke, he would mumble some inaudible comment. He also coached a trio I participated in, and he spoke no more audibly then than he did during my private lessons.

I couldn't understand why, apart from his reputation, the school had hired him. Then I learned that in every Stecker-student's life, the time came when the Master collected his thoughts, became blunt, and told the student exactly what his future would be. For me, the moment arrived on the third of November 1966. I was playing sections of the Brahms Paganini Variations, a fiendish piece on which I had spent many hours. When I finished, I saw him sit up.

"Very good," he said, squinting at me. "You have talents."

There was a pause. I waited. "Thank you," I said.

"You have a nice house?" he asked.

"A nice house? No."

"You should get a nice house somewhere," he said, taking his handkerchief out of his pocket and waving it at me. "With windows. Windows with a view."

I didn't like the drift of his remarks. "I can't afford a house," I said.

"You will. A nice house. For you and your family."

I resolved to get to the heart of this. "Professor," I asked, "what did you think of my playing?"

"Excellent," he said. "That piece is very difficult."

"Thank you."

"Yes, technically excellent," he said, and my heart began to pound. "Intelligent phrasing. Not much for me to say. Yes. That piece has many notes," he added, enjoying the non sequitur.

I nodded. "Many notes."

"And you hit all of them accurately. Good pedal and good discipline. I like how you hit the notes."

I was dangling on his string, a little puppet.

"Thousands of notes, I suppose," he said, staring at my forehead, which was beginning to get damp, "and you hit all of them. You only forgot one thing."

"What?"

"The passion!" he roared. "You forgot the passion! You always forget it! Where is it? Did you leave it at home? You never bring it with you! Never! I listen to you and think of a robot playing! A smart robot, but a robot! No passion! Never ever ever!" He stopped shouting long enough to sneeze. "You *should* buy a house. You know why?"

"Why?"

"Because the only way you will ever praise God is with a family, that's why! Not with this piano! You are a fine student," he wound up, "but you make me sick! Why do you make me sick?"

He waited for me to answer.

"*Why do you make me sick?*" he shouted. "Answer me!"

"How can I possibly answer you?"

"By articulating words in English! Be courageous! Offer a suggestion! Why do you make me sick?"

I waited for a minute, the longest minute of my life.

"Passion," I said at last. "You said there wasn't enough passion. I thought there was. Perhaps not."

He nodded. "No. You are right. No passion. A corruption of music itself. Your playing is gentle, too much good taste. To play the piano like a genius, you must have a bit of the fanatic. Just a bit. But it is essential. You have stubbornness and talent but no fanaticism. You don't have the salt on the rice. Without salt, the rice is inedible, no matter what its quality otherwise." He stood up. "I tell you this because sooner or later someone else will. You will have a life of disappointments if you stay in music. You may find a teacher who likes you. Good, good. *But you will never be taken up! Never!* You should buy a house, young man. With a beautiful view. Move to it. Don't stay here. You are close to success, but it is the difference between leaping the chasm and falling into it, one inch short. You are an inch short. You could come back for more lessons. You *could* graduate from here. But if you are truly intelligent, you will say goodbye. Goodbye." He looked down at the floor and did not offer me his hand.

I stood up and walked out of the room.

Becalmed, I drifted up and down the hallways of the building for half an hour. Then a friend of mine, a student of conducting from Bolivia, a Marxist named Juan Valparaiso, approached, and, ignoring my shallow breathing and cold sweat, started talking at once.

"Terrible, furious day!" he said.

"Yes."

"I am conducting *Benvenuto Cellini* overture this morning! All is going well until difficult flute entry. I instruct, with force, flutists. Soon all woodwinds are ignoring me." He raised his eyebrows and stroked his huge gaucho mustache. "Always! Always there are fascists in the woodwinds!"

"Fascists everywhere," I said.

"Horns bad, woodwinds worse. Demands of breath make for insanes. Pedro," he said, "you are appearing irresoluted. Sick?"

"Yes," I nodded. "Sick. I just came from Stecker. My playing makes *him* sick."

"He said that? That you are making him sick?"

"That's right. I play like a robot, he says."

"What will you do?" Juan asked me. "Kill him?"

"No." And then I knew. "I'm leaving the school."

"What? Is impossible!" Tears leaped instantly into Juan's eyes. "Cannot, Pedro. After one whipping? No! Must stick to it." He grabbed me by the shoulders. "Fascists put here on earth to break our hearts! Must live through. You cannot go." He looked around wildly. "Where could you go anyway?"

"I'm not sure," I said. "He told me I would never amount to anything. I think he's right. But I could do something else." To prove that I could imagine options, I said, "I could work for a newspaper. You know, music criticism."

"Caterpillars!" Juan shouted, his tears falling onto my shirt. "Failures! Pathetic lives! Cannot, cannot! Who would hire you?"

I couldn't tell him for six months, until I was given a job in Knoxville on a part-time trial basis. But by then I was no longer writing letters to my musician friends. I had become anonymous. I worked in Knoxville for two years, then in Louisville—a great city for music—until I moved here, to this city I shall never name, in the middle of New York State, where I bought a house with a beautiful view.

In my hometown, they still wonder what happened to me, but my smiling parents refuse to reveal my whereabouts.

Every newspaper has a command structure. Within that command structure, editors assign certain stories, but the writers must be given some freedom to snoop around and discover newsworthy material themselves. In this anonymous city, I was hired to review all the concerts of the symphony orchestra and to provide some hype articles during the week to boost the ticket sales for Friday's program. Since the owner of the paper was on the symphony board of trustees, writing about the orchestra and its programs was necessarily part of good journalistic citizenship. On my own, though, I initiated certain projects, wrote book reviews for the Sunday section, interviewed famous visiting musicians—some of them my ex-classmates—and during the summer I could fill in on all sorts of assignments, as long as I cleared what I did with the feature editor, Morris Cascadilla.

"You're the first serious musician we've ever had on the staff here," he announced to me when I arrived, suspicion and hope fighting for control on his face. "Just remember this: be clear and concise. Assume they've got intelligence but no information. After that, you're on your own, except that you should clear dicey stuff with me. And never forget the Maple Street angle."

The Maple Street angle was Cascadilla's equivalent to the Nixon administration's "How will it play in Peoria?" No matter what subject I wrote about, I was expected to make it relevant to Maple Street, the newspaper's mythical locus of middle-class values. I could write about electronic, aleatory, or post-Boulez music *if* I suggested that the city's daughters might be corrupted by it. Sometimes I found the Maple Street angle, and sometimes I couldn't. When I failed, Cascadilla would call me in, scowl at my copy, and mutter, "All the Juilliard graduates in town will love this." Nevertheless, the Maple Street angle was a spiritual exercise in humility, and I did my best to find it week after week.

When I first learned that the orchestra was scheduled to play Paul Hindemith's *Harmony of the World* symphony, I didn't think of Hindemith, but of Maple Street, that mythically harmonious place where I actually grew up.

Working on the paper left me some time for other activities. Unfortunately, there was nothing I knew how to do except play the piano and write reviews.

Certain musicians are very practical. Trumpet players (who love valves) tend to be good mechanics, and I have met a few composers who fly airplanes and can restore automobiles. Most performing violinists and pianists, however, are drained by the demands of their instruments and seldom learn how to do anything besides play. In daily life they are helpless and stricken. In midlife the smart ones force themselves to find hobbies. But the less fortunate come home to solitary apartments without pictures or other decorations, warm up their dinners in silence, read whatever books happen to be on the dinnertable, and then go to bed.

I am speaking of myself here, of course. As time passed, and the vacuum of my life made it harder to breathe, I required more work. I fancied that I was a tree, putting out additional leaves. I let it be known that I would play as an accompanist for voice students and other recitalists, if their schedules didn't interfere with my commitments for the paper.

One day I received a call at my desk. A quietly controlled female voice asked, "Is this Peter Jenkins?"

"Yes."

"Well," she said, as if she'd forgotten what she meant to tell me, "this is Karen Jensen. That's almost like Jenkins, isn't it?" I waited. "I'm a singer," she said, after a moment. "A soprano. I've just lost my accompanist and I'm planning on giving a recital in three months. They said you were available. Are you? And what do you charge?"

I told her.

"Isn't that kind of steep? That's kind of steep. Well, I suppose . . . I can use somebody else until just before, and then I can use you. They say you're good. And I've read your reviews. I really admire the way you write!"

I thanked her.

"You get so much information into your reviews! Sometimes, when I read you, I imagine what you look like. Sometimes a person can make a mental picture. I just wish the paper would publish a photo or something of you."

"They want to," I said, "but I asked them not to."

"Even your voice sounds like your writing!" she said excitedly. "I can see you in front of me now. Can you play Fauré and Schubert? I mean, is there any composer or style you don't like and won't play?"

"No," I said. "I play anything."

"That's *wonderful*!" she said, as if I had confessed to a remarkable tolerance. "Some accompanists are so picky. 'I won't do this, I won't do that.' Well, *one* I know is like that. Anyhow, could we meet soon? Do you sightread? Can we meet at the music school downtown? In a practice room? When are you free?"

I set up an appointment.

She was almost beautiful. Her deep eyes were accented by depressed bowls in quarter-moon shadows under them. Though she was only in her late twenties, she seemed slightly scorched by anxiety. She couldn't keep still. Her hands fluttered as they fixed her hair; she scratched nervously at her cheeks, and her eyes jumped every few seconds. Soon, however, she calmed down and began to look me in the eye, evaluating me. Then *I* turned away.

She wanted to test me out and had brought along her recital numbers, mostly standard fare: a Handel aria, Mozart, Schubert, and Fauré. The last set of songs, *Nine Epitaphs*, by an American composer I had never heard of, Theodore Chanler, was the only novelty.

"Who is this Chanler?" I asked, looking through the sheet music.

"I . . . I found it in the music library," she said. "I looked him up. He was born in Boston and he died in 1961. There's a recording by Phyllis Curtin. Virgil Thomson says these are maybe the best American art songs ever written."

"Oh."

"They're kind of, you know, lugubrious. I mean, they're all epitaphs written supposedly on tombstones, set to music. They're like portraits. I love them. Is it all right? Do you mind?"

"No, I don't mind."

We started through her program, beginning with Handel's "Un sospiretto d'un labbro pallido" from *Il Pastor fido*. I could immediately see why she was still in central New York State and why she would always be a student. She had a fine voice, clear and distinct, somewhat styled after Victoria de los Angeles (I thought), and her articulation was superb. If these achievements had been the whole story, she might have been a professional. But her pitch wobbled on sustained notes in a maddening way; the effect was not comic and would probably have gone unnoticed by most nonmusicians, but to me the result was harrowing. She could sing perfectly for several measures and then she would miss a note by a semitone, which drove an invisible finger-

nail into my scalp. It was as though a gypsy's curse descended every five or six seconds, throwing her off pitch;
then she was allowed to be a great singer until the curse
descended again. Her loss of pitch was so regularized that
I could see it coming and squirmed in anticipation. I felt as
though I were in the presence of one of God's more complicated pranks.

Her choice of songs highlighted her failings. Their delicate textures were constantly broken by her lapses. When
we arrived at the Chanler pieces, I thought I was accustomed to her, but I found I wasn't. The first song begins
with the following verse, written by Walter de la Mare, who
had crafted all the poems in archaic epitaph style:

> Here lyeth our infant, Alice Rodd;
> > She were so small
> > Scarce aught at all,
> But a mere breath of Sweetness sent from God.

The vocal line for "She were so small" consists of four notes,
the last two rising a half step from the two before them. To
work, the passage requires a deadeye accuracy of pitch:

Singing this line, Karen Jensen hit the D-sharp but missed
the E and skidded up uncontrollably to F-sharp, which
would sound all right to anyone who didn't have the music
in front of his nose, as I did. Only a fellow musician could
be offended.

Infuriated, I began to feel that I could *not* participate in a
recital with this woman. It would be humiliating to per-
form such lovely songs in this excruciating manner. I stopped
playing, turned to her to tell her that I could not continue
after all, and then I saw her bracelet.

I am not, on the whole, especially observant, a failing
that probably accounts for my having missed the bracelet
when we first met. But I saw it now: five silver canaries
dangled down quietly from it, and as it slipped back and
forth, I saw her wrist and what I suddenly realized *would*
be there: the parallel lines of her madness, etched in scar
tissue.

The epitaphs finished, she asked me to work with her,
and I agreed. When we shook hands, the canaries shook
in tiny vibrations, as if pleased with my dutiful kindness,
my charity, toward their mad mistress.

Though Paul Hindemith's reputation once equalled Stra-
vinsky's and Bartók's, it suffered after his death in 1963 an
almost complete collapse. Only two of his orchestral works,
the *Symphonic Metamorphoses on Themes of Weber* and the
Mathis der Maler symphony, are played with any frequency,
thanks in part to their use of borrowed tunes. One hears
his woodwind quintets and choral pieces now and then,
but the works of which he was most proud—the ballet *No-
bilissima Visione*, *Das Marienleben* (a song cycle), and the opera *Harmonie die Welt*—have fallen into total obscurity.

The reason for Hindemith's sudden loss of reputation was
a mystery to me; I had always considered his craftsman-
ship if not his inspiration to be first-rate. When I saw that
the *Harmony of the World* symphony, almost never played,
would be performed in our anonymous city, I told Cascadilla that I wanted to write a story for that week on how
fame was gained and lost in the world of music. He thought

that subject might be racy enough to interest the tone-deaf
citizens of leafy and peaceful Maple Street, where no one
is famous, if I made sure the story contained "the human
element."

I read up on Hindemith, played his piano music, and
listened to the recordings. I slowly found the music to be
technically astute but emotionally arid, as if some problem
of purely local interest kept the composer's gaze safely below the horizon. Technocratic and oddly timid, his work
reminded me of a model train chugging through a tiny town
inhabited only by models of people. In fact, Hindemith did
have a lifelong obsession with train sets: in Berlin, his collection took up three rooms, and the composer wrote elab-
orate timetables so that the toys wouldn't collide.

But if Hindemith had a technocrat's intelligence, he also
believed in the necessity of universal participation in musical activities. Listening was not enough. Even nonmusi-
cal citizens could learn to sing and play, and he wrote music expressly for this purpose. He seems to have known
that passive, drugged listening was a side-effect of totali-
tarian environments and that elitist composers such as
Schoenberg were engaged in antisocial Faustian projects
that would bewilder and ultimately infuriate most audiences, leaving them isolated and thus eager to be drugged
by a musical superman.

As the foremost anti-Nietzschean German composer of
his day, therefore, Hindemith left Germany when his works
could not be performed, thanks to the Third Reich; wrote
textbooks with simple exercises; composed a requiem in
memory of Franklin Roosevelt, using a text by Walt Whitman; and taught students, not all of them talented, in An-
kara, New Haven, and Buffalo ("this caricature of a town").
As he passed through late middle age, he turned to a project he had contemplated all his life, an opera based on the
career of the German astronomer Johannes Kepler, author
of *De Harmonice Mundi*. This opera, a summary of Hindemith's ideas, would be called *Harmony of the World*. Hindemith worked out the themes first in a symphony, which
bore the same title as the opera, and completed it in 1951.

The more I thought about this project, the more it seemed anachronistic. Who believed in world harmony in 1951? Or thereafter? Such a symphony would have to pass beyond technical sophistication into divine inspiration, which Hindemith had never shown any evidence of possessing.

It occurred to me that Hindemith's lifelong sanity had perhaps given way in this case, toppled not by despair (as is conventional) but by faith in harmony.

For the next rehearsal, I drove to Karen Jensen's apartment, where there was, she said, a piano. I'd become curious about the styles of her insanity: I imagined a hamster cage in the kitchen, a doll-head mobile in the living room, and mottos written with different colored inks on memo pads tacked up everywhere on the walls.

She greeted me at the door without her bracelet. When I looked at her wrist, she said, "Hmmm. I see that you noticed. A memento of adolescent despair." She sighed. "But it does frighten people off. Once you've tried to do something like that, people don't really trust you. I don't know why exactly. They don't want your blood on their hands or something. Well, come on in."

I was struck first by her forthrightness and secondly by her tiny apartment. Its style was much like the style in my house. She owned an attractive but worn-down sofa, a sideboard that supported an antique clock, one chair, a glass-top dinner table, and one nondescript poster on the wall. Trying to keep my advantage, I looked hard for telltale signs of insanity but found none. The piano was off in the corner, almost hidden, unlike those in the parlors back home.

"Very nice," I said.

"Well, thanks," she said. "It's not much. I'd like something bigger, but . . . where I work, I'm an administrative assistant, and they don't pay me very much. So that's why I live like a snail here. It's hardly big enough to move around in, right?" She wasn't looking at me. "I mean, I could almost pick it up and carry it away."

I nodded. "You just don't think like a rich person," I said,

trying to be hearty. "They like to expand. They need room.
Big houses, big cars, fat bodies."

"Oh, I know!" she said, laughing. "My uncle . . . would
you like to stay for dinner? You look like you need a good
meal. I mean, after the rehearsal. You're just skin and bones,
Pet— . . . may I call you Peter?"

"Sure." I sat down on the sofa and tried to think up an
excuse. "I really can't stay, Miss Jensen. I have another rehearsal to go to later tonight. I wish I could."

"That's not it, is it?" she asked suddenly, looking down
at me. "I don't believe you. I bet it's something else. I bet
you're afraid of me."

"Why should I be afraid of you?"

She smiled and shrugged. "That's all right. You don't have
to say anything. I know how it goes." She laughed once
more, faintly. "I never found a man who could handle it.
They want to show you *their* scars, you know? They don't
want to see any on you. If they discover any, they just run."
She slapped her right hand into her forehead and then ran
her fingers through her hair. "Well, shit, I didn't mean to
do this *at all*! I mean, I admire you so much and everything,
and here I am running on like this. I guess we should get
down to business, right? Since I'm paying you by the hour."

I smiled professionally and went to her piano.

Beneath the high culture atmosphere that surrounds
them, art songs have one subject: love. The permutations
of love (lust, solitude, and loss) are present in abundance,
of course, but for the most part they are simple vehicles for
the expression of that one emotion. I was reminded of this
as I played through the piano parts. As much as I concen-
trated on the music in front of me, I couldn't help but notice that my employer stood next to the piano, singing the
words sometimes toward me, sometimes away. She was
rather courageously forcing eye contact on me. She kept
this up for an hour and a half until we came to the Chanler
settings, when at last she turned slightly, singing to the
walls.

As before, her voice broke out of control every five seconds, giving isolated words all the wrong shadings. The
only way to endure it, I discovered, was to think of her

singing as a postmodern phenomenon with its own con-
ventions and rules. As the victim of necessity rather than
accident, Karen Jensen was tolerable.

> Here sleep I,
> Susannah Fry,
> No one near me,
> No one nigh:
> Alone, alone
> Under my stone,
> Dreaming on,
> Still dreaming on:
> Grass for my valance
> And coverlid,
> Dreaming on
> As I always did.
> "Weak in the head?"
> Maybe. Who knows?
> Susannah Fry
> Under the rose.

There she was, facing away from me, burying Susannah
Fry, and probably her own past and career into the bargain.
When we were done, she asked, "Sure you won't stay?"
"No, I don't think so."
"You really haven't another engagement, do you?"
"No," I admitted.
"I didn't think so. You were scared of me the moment
you walked in the door. You thought I'd be crazy." She
waited. "After all, only ugly girls live alone, right? And I'm
not ugly."
"No, you aren't," I said. "You're quite attractive."
"Do you think so?" she asked, brightening. "It's so nice
to hear that from you, even if you're just paying a compliment. I mean, it still means *something*." Then she surprised
me. As I stood in the doorway, she got down on her knees
in front of me and bowed her head in the style of one of
her songs. "Please stay," she asked. Immediately she stood
up and laughed. "But don't feel obliged to."
"Oh, no," I said, returning to her living room, "I've just
changed my mind. Dinner sounds like a good idea."

After she had served and we had started to eat, she looked up at me and said, "You know, I'm not completely good." She paused. "At singing."

"What?" I stopped chewing. "Yes, you are. You're all right."

"Don't lie. I know I'm not. You know I'm not. Come on: let's at least be honest. I think I have certain qualities of musicality, but my pitch is . . . you know. Uneven. You probably think it's awfully vain of me to put on these recitals. With nobody but friends and family coming."

"No, I don't."

"Well, I don't care what you say. It's . . . hmm, I don't know. People encourage me. And it's a discipline. Music's finally a discipline that rewards you. Privately, though. Well, that's what my mother says."

Carefully, I said, "She may be right."

"Who cares if she is?" she laughed, her mouth full of food. "I enjoy doing it. Like I enjoy doing this. Listen, I don't want to seem forward or anything, but are you married?"

"No."

"I didn't think so." She picked up a string bean and eyed it suspiciously. "Why aren't you? You're not ugly. In fact you're all-right looking. You obviously haven't been crazy. Are you gay or something?"

"No."

"No," she agreed, "you don't look gay. You don't even look very happy. You don't look very anything. Why is that?"

"I should be offended by this line of questioning."

"But you're not. You know why? Because I'm interested in you. I hardly know you, but I like you, what I can see. Don't you have any trust?"

"Yes," I said finally.

"So answer my question. Why don't you look very anything?"

"Do you want to hear what my piano teacher once said?" I asked. "He said I wasn't enough of a fanatic. He said that to be one of the great ones you have to be a tiny bit crazy. Touched. And he said I wasn't. And when he said it, I knew all along he was right. I was waiting for someone to say

what I already knew, and he was the one. I was too much
a good citizen, he said. I wasn't possessed."
    She rose, walked around the table to where I was sitting,
and stood in front of me, looking down at my face. I knew
that whatever she was going to do had been picked up, in
attitude, from one of her songs. She touched the back of
my arm with two fingers on her right hand. "Well," she
said, "maybe you aren't possessed, but what would you
think of me as another possession?"

    In 1618, at the age of seventy, Katherine Kepler, the mother
of Johannes Kepler, was put on trial for witchcraft. The records indicate that her personality was so deranged, so deeply
offensive to all, that if she were alive today she would *still*
be called a witch. One of Kepler's biographers, Angus Armitage, notes that she was "evil-tempered" and possessed
an interest in unnamed "outlandish things." Her trial lasted,
on and off, for three years; by 1621, when she was acquit-
ted, her personality had disintegrated completely. She died
the following year.
    At the age of six, Kepler's son Frederick died of small-
pox. A few months later, Kepler's wife, Barbara, died of
typhus. Two other children, Henry and Susanna, had died
in infancy.
    Like many others of his age, Kepler spent much of his
adult life cultivating favor from the nobility. He was habit-
ually penniless and was often reduced, as his correspondence shows, to begging for handouts. He was the victim
of religious persecution, though luckier in this regard than
some.
    After he married for a second time, three more children
died in infancy, a statistic that in theory carries less emotional weight than one might think, given the accepted levels of infant mortality for that era.
    In 1619, despite the facts cited above, Kepler published
De Harmonice Mundi, a text in which he set out to establish
the correspondence between the laws of harmony and the
disposition of planets in motion. In brief, Kepler argued
that certain intervals, such as the octave, major and minor
sixths, and major and minor thirds, were pleasurable, while

other intervals were not. History indicated that mankind
had always regarded certain intervals as unpleasant. Feeling that this set of universal tastes pointed to immutable
laws, Kepler sought to map out the pleasurable intervals
geometrically, and then to transfer that geometrical pattern
to the order of the planets. The velocity of the planets, rather
than their strict placement, constituted the harmony of the
spheres. This velocity provided each planet with a note,
what Armitage called a "term in a mathematically determined relation."

> In fact, each planet performed a short musical scale, set down
> by Kepler in staff notation. The length of the scale depended
> upon the eccentricity of the orbit; and its limiting notes could
> generally be shown to form a concord (except for Venus and
> the Earth with their nearly circular orbits, whose scales were
> of very constricted range) . . . at the Creation . . . complete
> concord prevailed and the morning stars sang together.

We began to eat dinner together. Accustomed to solitude, we did not always engage in conversation. I would
read the newspaper or ink in letters on my geometrically
patterned crossword puzzles at my end of the table, while
Karen would read detective novels or *Time* at hers. If she
had cooked, I would clear and wash the dishes. If I had
cooked, she did the cleaning. Experience and disappointments had made us methodical. She told me that she had
once despised structured experiences governed by timetables, but that after several manic-depressive episodes, she
had learned to love regularity. This regularity included taking lithium at the same time—to the minute—each day.

The season being summer, we would pack towels and
swimming suits after dinner and drive out to one of several
public beaches, where we would swim until darkness came
on. On calm evenings, Karen would drop her finger in the
water and watch the waves lap outward. I favored imma-
ture splashing, or grabbing her by the arm and whirling
her around me until I released her and she would spin back
and fall into the water, laughing as she sank. One evening,
we found a private beach, two hundred feet of sand all to

ourselves, on a lake thirty miles out of town. Framed on both sides by woods and well-hidden from the highway, this beach had the additional advantage of being unpatrolled. We had no bathhouse in which to change, however, so Karen instructed me not to look as she walked about fifty feet away to a spot where she undressed and put on her suit.

Though we had been intimate for at least a week, I had still not seen her naked: like a good Victorian, she demanded that the shades be drawn, the lights be out, and the covers be pulled discreetly over us. But now, with the same methodical thoroughness, she wanted me to see her, so I looked, despite her warnings. She was bent over, under the tree boughs, the evening light breaking through the leaves and casting broken gold bands on her body. Her arms were delicate, the arms of a schoolgirl, I thought, an impression heightened by the paleness of her skin; but her breasts were full, at first making me think of Rubens's women, then of Renoir's, then of nothing at all. Slowly, knowing I was watching her, she pinned her hair up. Not her breasts or arms, but that expression of vague contentment as she looked out toward the water, away from me: *that* made me feel a tingling below my heart, somewhere in an emotional center near my stomach. I wanted to pick her up and carry her somewhere, but with my knees wobbly it was all I could do to make my way over to where she stood and take her in my arms before she cried out. "Jesus," she said, shivering, "you gave me a surprise." I kissed her, waiting for inspiration to direct me on what to do next: pick her up? Carry her? Make love to her on the sand? Wade into the water with her and swim out to the center of the bay, where we would drown together in a Lawrentian love-grip? But then we broke the kiss; she put on her swimsuit like a good citizen, and we swam for the usual fifteen minutes in silence. Afterward, we changed back into our clothes and drove home, muttering small talk. Behavior inspired by and demonstrating love embarrassed both of us. When I told her that she was beautiful and that I loved her, she patted me on the cheek and said, "Aw, how nice. You always try to say the right thing."

The Maple Street angle for *Harmony of the World* ran as follows: SYMPHONY OF FAITH IN A FAITHLESS AGE. Hindemith, I said, wished to confound the skeptics by composing a monument of faith. In an age of organized disharmony, of political chaos, he stood at the barricades defending tonality and traditional musical form. I carefully avoided any specific discussion of the musical materials of the symphony, which in the Schott orchestral score looked overcomplex and melodically ugly. From what I could tell from a sightreading, Hindemith had employed stunning technique in order to disguise his lack of inspiration, though I did not say so in print. Instead, I wrote that the symphony's failure to win public support was probably the result of Hindemith's refusal to use musical gimmicks on the one hand and sticky-sweet melodies on the other. I wrote that he had not been dismayed by the bad reviews *Harmony of the World* (both the symphony and the opera) had received, which was untrue. I said he was a man of integrity. I did not say that men of integrity are often unable to express joy when the occasion demands. Cascadilla liked my article. "This guy sounds like me," he said, reading my copy. "I respect him." The article ran five days before the concert and was two pages away from the religion-and-faith section. Not long after, the symphony ticket office called me to say that my piece had caused a rush of ticket orders from ordinary folk, nonconcert types, who wanted to hear this "religious symphony." The woman from the business office thanked me for my trouble. "Let's hope they like it," I said.

"Of course they will," she assured me. "You've told them to."

But they didn't. Despite all the oratory in the symphony, it was as spiritually dead as a lampshade. I could see why Hindemith had been shocked by the public reaction. Our audience applauded politely in discouragement, and then I heard an unusual sound for this anonymous city: one man, full of fun and conviction, booing loudly from the balcony. Booing the harmony of the world! He must be a Satanist! Didn't intentions mean anything? So what if the harmony and joy were all counterfeit? The conductor came out for a bow, smiled at the booing man, and very soon the applause died away. I left the hall, feeling responsible. Arriving at the paper, I wrote a review of crushing dullness that reeked of bad faith. Goddamn Hindemith! Here he was, claiming to have seen God's workings, and they sounded like the workings of a steam engine or a trolley car. A fake symphony, with optimism the composer did not feel! I decided (but did not write) that *Harmony of the World* was just possibly the largest, most misconceived fiasco in modern music's history. It was a symphony that historically could not be written by a man who was constitutionally not equipped to write it. In my review, I kept a civil pen: I said that the performance lacked "luster," "a certain necessary glow."

"I'm worried about the recital tomorrow."

"Aw, don't worry. Here, kiss me. Right here."

"Aren't you listening? I'm worried."

"*I'm* singing. You're just accompanying me. Nobody's going to notice you. Move over a little, would you? Yeah, there. That pillow was forcing my head against the wall."

"Why aren't you worried?"

"Why should I be worried? I don't want to worry. I want to make love. Isn't that better than worrying?"

"Not if I'm worried."

"People won't notice you. By the way, have you paid attention to the fact that when I kiss you on the stomach, you get goosebumps?"

"Yes. I think you're taking this pretty lightly. I mean, it's almost unprofessional."

"That's because I'm an amateur. A one hundred percent amateur. Always and totally. Even at this. But that doesn't mean I don't have my moments. Mmmmmm. That's better."

"I thought it would maybe help. But listen. I'm still worried."

"Uhhhh. Oh, wait a minute. Wait a minute. Oh, I get it."

"What?"

"I get it. You aren't worried about yourself. You're worried about me."

Forty people attended her recital, which was sponsored
by the city university's music school, in which Karen was a
sometime student. Somehow we made our way through
the program, but when we came to the Chanler settings, I
suddenly wanted Karen to sing them perfectly. I wanted
an angel to descend and to take away the gypsy's curse.
But she sang as she always had—off pitch—and when she
came to "Ann Poverty," I found myself in that odd region
between rage and pity.

> Stranger, here lies
> Ann Poverty;
> Such was her name
> And such was she.
> May Jesu pity
> Poverty.

But I was losing my capacity for pity.

In the green room, her forty friends came back to congratulate her. I met them. They were all very nice. She smiled
and laughed: there would be a party in an hour. Would I
go? I declined. When we were alone, I said I was going
back to my place.

"Why?" she asked. "Shouldn't you come to my party?
You're my lover after all. That *is* the word."

"Yes. But I don't want to go with you."

"Why?"

"Because of tonight's concert, that's why."

"What about it?"

"It wasn't very good, was it? I mean, it just wasn't."

"I thought it was all right. A few slips. It was pretty much
what I was capable of. All those people said they liked it."

"Those people don't matter!" I said, my eyes watering
with anger. "Only the music matters. Only the music is
betrayed; they aren't. They don't know about pitch, most
of them. I mean, Jesus, they aren't genuine musicians, so
how would they know? Do you really think what we did
tonight was good? It wasn't! It was a travesty! We ruined
those songs! How can you stand to do that?"

"I don't ruin them. I sing them adequately. I project feeling. People get pleasure from them. That's enough."

"It's awful," I said, feeling the ecstatic lift-off into rage. "You're so close to being good, but you *aren't* good. Who cares what those ignoramuses think? They don't know what notes you're *supposed* to hit. It's that goddamn slippery pitch of yours. You're killing those songs. You just *drop* them like watermelons on the stage! It makes me sick! I couldn't have gone on for another day listening to you and your warbling! I'd die first."

She looked at me and nodded, her mouth set in a half-moue, half-smile of nonsurprise. There may have been tears in her eyes, but I didn't see them. She looked at me as if she were listening hard to a long-distance call. "You're tired of me," she said.

"I'm not tired of you. I'm tired of hearing you sing! Your voice makes my flesh crawl! Do you know why? Can you tell me why you make me sick? Why do you make me sick? Never mind. I'm just glad this is over."

"You don't look glad. You look angry."

"And you look smug. Listen, why don't you go off to your party? Maybe there'll be a talent scout there. Or roses flung riotously at you. But don't give a recital like this again, please, okay? It's a public disgrace. It offends music. It offends *me*."

I turned my back on her and walked out to my car.

After the failure of *Harmony of the World*, Hindemith went on a strenuous tour that included Scandinavia. In Oslo, he was rehearsing the Philharmonic when he blinked his bright blue eyes twice, turned to the concertmaster, and said, "I don't know where I am." They took him away to a hospital; he had suffered a nervous breakdown.

I slept until noon, having nothing to do at the paper and no reason to get up. At last, unable to sleep longer, I rose and walked to the kitchen to make coffee. I then took my cup to the picture window and looked down the hill to the trees of the conservation area, the view Stecker had once told me I should have.

The figure of a woman was hanging from one of the trees,

a noose around her neck. I dropped my coffee cup and the liquid spilled out over my feet.

I ran out the back door in my pajamas and sprinted painfully down the hill's tall grass toward the tree. I was fifty feet away when I saw that it wasn't Karen, wasn't in fact a woman at all, but an effigy of sorts, with one of Karen's hats, a pillow head, and a dress hanging over a broomstick skeleton. Attached to the effigy was a note:

> In the old days, this might have been me. Not anymore. Still, I thought it'd make you think. And I'm not giving up singing, either. By the way, what your playing lacks is not fanaticism, but concentration. You can't seem to keep your mind on one thing for more than a minute at a time. *I* notice things too. You aren't the only reviewer around here. Take good care of this doll, okay?
>
> XXXXXXX,
> Karen

I took the doll up and dropped it in the clothes closet, where it has remained to this hour.

Hindemith's biographer, Geoffrey Skelton, writes, "[On the stage] the episodic scenes from Kepler's life fail to achieve immediate dramatic coherence, and the basic theme remains obscure . . . "

She won't, of course, see me again. She won't talk to me on the phone, and she doesn't answer my letters. I am quite lucidly aware of what I have done. And I go on seeing doubles and reflections and wave motion everywhere. There is symmetry, harmony, after all. I suppose I should have been nice to her. That, too, is a discipline. I always tried to be nice to everyone else.

On his deathbed, Hindemith has Kepler sing:

> *Und muss sehn am End:*
> *Die grosse Harmonie, das is der Tod.*
> *Absterben is, sie zu bewirken, not.*
> *Im Leben hat sie keine Statte.*
>
> Now, at the end, I see it:
> The great harmony, it is death.

To find it, we must die.
In life it has no place.

Hindemith's words may be correct. But Dante says that
the residents of limbo, having never been baptised, will
not see the face of God, despite their having committed no
sin, no active fault. In their fated locale, they sigh, which
keeps the air "forever trembling." No harmony for them,
these guiltless souls. Through eternity, the residents of
limbo—where one can imagine oneself if one cannot stand
to imagine any part of hell—experience one of the most
shocking of all the emotions that Dante names: "duol senza
martíri," grief without torment. These sighs are rather like
the sounds one hears drifting from front porches in small
towns on soft summer nights.

The Crank

After his second divorce, no one would talk to him for a while. The people who hadn't liked the formality of his first wife had really taken to the ruddy charm of the second one, so that when that marriage also failed, he had had to shoulder a considerable part of the blame himself. His friends took their time returning his calls. Whenever he met them on the street, they were eager to get to their next appointment, and they looked at him with a mild, intelligent disgust, as if he were a convert to a new unfashionable psychotherapy from California.

All he had done at first was divorce his wife, give her the custody of the two kids, and marry his girlfriend. This girlfriend, Alicia, had a soft voice, blue eyes, thick blond hair, and an apartment full of houseplants that covered the windowsills. She did aerobic dancing five times a week to Boz Scaggs, wearing leg warmers over purple leotards. What made him take the final leap was the way she would sing to him after they made love. She sang the same eight or nine songs very softly close to his face and ran her fingers through his hair. It broke his resolve.

So he divorced his wife as quickly as he could and married Alicia. He left most of his old belongings at home and moved into her apartment. This is a new leaf, he thought. They were going to find some other place, but in a short time she grew annoyed at his visible guilt. She lectured him about the dangers of self-punishment and quoted Bob Seger. When she took a new lover, he moved out and found a one-bedroom apartment that looked out over a small unnamed city park. He went back to the same divorce lawyer he had had the first time, and when he came home he would stare at his possessions: a bed, a TV tray, a lamp, a reclining chair, and a piano. After the second divorce was final, he purchased a new reliable television set.

He had die-hard friends, but they served him pork roast and not very good wines at dinner, and most of them were still seeing his first wife socially, trying not to take sides. His recent glaring failures in judgment made conversation troublesome; mostly they talked about movies and expensive luxury brands of ice cream.

As for his two boys, he picked them up on Saturday mornings and took them to his apartment, where they watched programs on the new television and worked on model airplanes and funny cars on newspapers spread out across the living room floor. They ate hotdogs, and the air smelled of glue. As winter came on, seeing they had nothing on their heads, he bought them caps with soft brown muffled earflaps. One Sunday night, one half hour after he had dropped them off at the house where he himself had lived for fourteen years, he actually threw up in his own bathroom under the stress of grief.

Weekdays, he came home from work at the real estate office, where he was doing a manically energetic job of holding clients and selling them anything he wanted them to buy. He shut the curtains, turned on the TV, put on his jogging suit, and ran around the park twice. He liked the TV to be on when he came in. He showered and ate dinner. This was in early December. He read the newspapers while he ate. He tried hard not to think about things. After dinner he wanted to call somebody. The telephone sat on the floor on top of the city directory. But even trustworthy people had a way of making pronouncements over the phone that they didn't have the nerve to say in person. The last caller he had talked to, his favorite aunt, had said, "One divorce is human. Two divorces makes you kind of special but not real special. One more, and it's all they're ever going to remember about your whole life."

He read a column in the life-and-leisure section of the newspaper about not being a victim of circumstance. He glanced up and checked his apartment. It was the interior decoration of a known victim. After getting into his car, he drove out to a boarded-up A & W Root Beer stand where Christmas trees were sold by a fat man who smoked cigars. He bought a Douglas fir small enough to fit in his trunk. On the way back, he stopped at Ace Hardware and purchased lights, sixteen pink and blue ornaments, and tinsel.

He carried the tree and decorations up to his apartment, turned on the Monday night football game, and then realized that he had forgotten to buy a tree stand. Joe Montana was throwing a pass to Renaldo Nehemiah; immobilized, he stared at the television set, unsure whether he supported the 49ers or their opponents, Tampa Bay. He turned the sound down and went to the piano. The Christmas tree lay on its side near the window, and the brown bags stood up straight next to the reclining chair. The particles of snow on the tree began to melt and drip into the carpeting. Playing the piano, he watched the television set, admiring the green of the artificial turf. He felt slightly sick. At that point the telephone rang.

"Hello," he said, moving the brown bags aside.

"Hello," the voice said.

"Who is this?" he asked. There was a silence. "Who is this?"

"Just someone," the caller told him. "I had expected a woman."

"Then you have the wrong number."

"Maybe I don't," the voice said. "This might not be the wrong number."

"Who do you want?" he asked. "I'm the only person who lives here." The 49ers had just scored. "What do you want?"

"I had expected a woman," the voice repeated. "In the new phonebook here it says R. Brennan. Initials usually mean a woman."

"Who is this?"

"I'm one of those people who calls," the voice said. "One of those cranks."

"Oh."

"You don't care?" the voice asked.

"Actually I don't," he said. "It's all the same to me, whoever you are." He waited, watching the football game. Ray Wersching's kick went up between the posts. "The R is for Robert," he said after a moment's thought.

"Glad to meet you," the crank said. "Call me Oscar."

"Sure." There was an absentminded pause. "Do we have anything to talk about?" He waited. "Why do you make crank calls?"

"That's a good question," the voice said. "I don't breathe or do obscenities like the others. Me, I just like to talk. I'd rather talk to women, but I'll talk to men. The trouble, I mean the real technical trouble, is keeping people on the line. Usually they hang up right away. That's a sign. They're busy, they've got family, they don't want anything weird. Anyone who stays on as long as you, well, that's a sign too. A bad sign for you, a good one for me. Like I say, I'll talk to anyone. For example, I'll talk to you."

"Okay."

"What're you doing now?" the crank asked.

"Putting up a Christmas tree. But I forgot to buy a stand, so I can't. And I'm watching the football game."

"Well, there you are," the crank said. "So am I. The 49ers just pulled ahead. I thought they would. You a betting man?"

"No. No, I don't think so."

"Too bad." There was another pause. "We're both watching this game here, and you don't want to put any money on it?"

"No. I got alimony payments," Robert said.

"That's an interesting viewpoint," the crank observed. "Why don't you have a Christmas tree stand. You said you had a tree but no stand." He sometimes left the rising inflection off questions.

"I don't have anything," he told the caller. "I've been through two divorces and I don't have anything. Just look. Just look around at this apartment. Do you see anything here? No. That's how it is now." He hung up and unplugged the telephone from its wall socket.

An insomniac, he woke up at three o'clock. He dressed, drove to an all-night drug store and bought a green-and-red stand. All the women in the drug store looked away from him. He thought, I'm one of them, looking for bargains at three in the morning. A man doesn't have to shave to come down and do this; he doesn't have to put on deodorant. He paid at the cash register and drove home listening to a beautiful music station. In the living room he twisted the stand's screws into the trunk of the tree, put on the lights and ornaments, but left the tinsel for later. He left the lights burning all night in front of the window as a charm.

He had successfully completed a closing with a single-parent client later in the week and offered to take her out to dinner. They went to a dark restaurant downtown where the tables were covered with white linen and the waiters bowed with their feet together. They finished a bottle of Zinfandel, and the client leaned over the table toward him. At once he felt distinctly sick. "Do you ever notice," he asked, trying to fight off nausea, "how sticky it is to tell about anybody? About whether you care for them or not? You're single, but it's something most regular people don't realize at all. One minute they're nice—you know, like people are—going shopping or whatever, and the next minute they're writing contracts with binding clauses. I wasn't told how to prepare for divorces. Remember? Your parents don't tell you. Nothing prepares you. Wow, I shouldn't talk like this. The smart thing to do would be to shut up." He could not stop talking. "I shouldn't say any more. It's funny: do you remember the first time you met someone you loved and then hated later? I do. Sometimes it's all you *do* remember. That's how they get to you. You remember the perfume especially, especially that, and the weather and how the car smelled and what they were playing on the radio. But you don't remember what you said. No, the other person always remembers that, and it goes into the contract. I wish I could stop saying this. I'm not used to living alone or drinking so much wine. Can I take you home after dinner? I'm not like this at all. I'm very straight. I certainly haven't screwed up on the job or misled you in any way. You have to admit that."

He drove the client back to her apartment and walked her to the door. There, her last words were, "Honey, you shouldn't drink. I know the name of a good therapist. You want his number?"

When he returned to his place he turned on the Christmas tree. He sat on the sofa staring at it with a glazed, dumbfounded expression while he drank Scotch. Something was amiss with the tree. It had a brooding, Germanic quality, as if it had been shipped from the Black Forest. Although he had poured water into the stand, the tree was dry, and its needles fell with a whispery rustling sound through the branches onto the bed sheet he had put on the floor around the base. He noticed belatedly that the tree's failure in raising his spirits had something to do with the absence of Christmas gifts. He had already given his boys their presents, and now they had left town with their mother, vacationing in Disneyland, the California one. "You shouldn't put up trees," he said to the floor, "if you aren't going to get any presents." His boys had given him after-shave, an expensive ballpoint pen, and a digital bedside clock. The phone was ringing, he suddenly noticed.

"Good evening," he said. Then he added, apologetically, "Hello."

"You're drunk," the voice said. "Why are you drunk?"

"Why are you sober?" he asked. "Who is this? Is this that nut who called me before?"

"Yes," the voice said. "Oscar. You may call me Oscar." He waited. "You're Robert, aren't you? May I call you Robert?"

"No," he said. "No one calls me Robert. They all call me Mr. Brennan. All the people who called me Robert have gone on vacation for the holidays. No one by that name lives here."

"I don't like the sound of this," the crank said. "What's the matter with you. Why are you so morose?"

"None of your business."

"That's true. Hang up." He waited. "I said, if it's none of my business, hang up. After all, I'm just a crank."

He held on to the telephone, staring at the Christmas tree. The tiny lights blinked. It made him think of a department store. "What do you want?" he asked. "You must want something. Everyone does."

"I explained all that to you," the crank said. "I think I can help you. You need to get into the spirit of things. You *aren't* in the spirit of things. I don't get that sense from you. This is more like an emergency. I propose a meeting. There are only so many things you can do on the phone. I suggest we meet in that park in front of your apartment. You don't

have to invite me in. I'm not dangerous. I figure, maybe
we should meet. Why not? Name a time. I'll be there."

"This is ridiculous," Robert said. He did not hang up.
"What if you . . . oh, who cares? Late tomorrow afternoon,
when I get home from work, around six o'clock. It'll be
dark by then. How will I recognize you? And where will
we meet? It's not a big park, but it's—"

"—I'll be sitting on a bench," the crank said. "Aren't you
frightened of me. Usually people don't set up a meeting so
fast with someone they don't know. This is quite unusual."

"What the hell," he said. "Who cares? That's my thinking."

"Oh," the crank said, and there was a long silence before
he hung up.

During the day he seldom thought about his appointment at the park bench, but by the time he arrived home
he wanted someone to talk to, and then felt better about
meeting a man he had never seen. After washing his face,
he put on his overcoat again and, being late, ran downstairs and plunged out into the darkness. Streetlights gave
an icicle brightness to the exterior of the park, but its interior was a hollow inky black. The snow failed to lighten the
path, and he slowed down, afraid of stretches of ice and
long tunnels of darkness. His ears burned from the cold,
and his eyes watered. Walking in darkness, on ice packed
from snow, he remembered a park bench in front of him
and to his right. All around him the darkness collaborated
with the cold, intensifying it. In return, the cold made the
darkness even more dark. He reached the bench before quite
apprehending that it was there or that there was a man
sitting on it. He tried to stop, slid on the ice, then turned
around.

The crank sat on the bench, enveloped in darkness. Robert could detect the outlines of his earflaps, muffler, and
furry overcoat. He saw that the crank was wearing glasses,
and he heard the sound of chewing. There was a smell in
the air, unmistakable, of candy.

"Howdy," the crank said. "You're late."

"Got caught in traffic," he said. "You're eating."

"Raisinets," the crank said, holding out the box. "Want some?"

"No thanks."

"Whenever I go to the movies, I always buy lots of candy. You can't always get that stuff at the grocery store. You know, theater candy: Jordan Almonds, Milk Duds, Goobers, Jujyfruits, red licorice, the fancy kind with the barber-pole swirls. Strawberry Twizzlers, they're called. Drugstores don't carry them. And of course Raisinets. I eat candy when I make phone calls. It disguises my voice."

"Oh."

"I see you're not interested."

"No, not especially."

"Listen," the crank said. "I understand what you're going through." Robert heard the crank's boots tapping out some rhythm on the ice. "You think you're so special. Well, you're nobody special, and neither is anyone else. It's time you got interested in things again. I ought to know. I'm here to help you."

"How?"

"Well, for example," the crank said, then stopped. He tilted his head back, and Robert saw the moon reflected and split on his bifocals. "This weekend the Vikings are playing the Detroit Lions. You got an opinion about the outcome?"

"Where's it being played?"

"You certainly *are* out of it," the crank said. "Here. At the Metrodome."

"Vikings by fourteen," Robert said. "But who cares?"

"Let's start with you. Put some money on it. A hundred dollars. I'll do the charity part and take the Lions and I won't even demand the fourteen points it'd take to make this a fair bet. My mother, may she rest in peace, would be ashamed of me for this. I'm playing the sucker for you. Well, all right. It's a sacrificial bet. I might as well give you that money right now, hand it over in cash. I'm willing to let my faith in Bud Grant slip down the drain this one time, for your sake."

"All right. It's a deal."

The man on the bench transferred the Raisinets to his

left hand and held up his right hand. Robert took off his glove and shook the hand held toward him. It was neither warm nor cold.

"You got yourself a wager," the man said. "Now pay attention. This is Wednesday. I will be here next Sunday night to pay off or collect. You come see me and we'll set up something for the Monday night game. Are you listening?"

"Yes," Robert said. "I'll be out here. Same time?"

"Don't be a moron," the crank said. He stood up and walked off, leaving behind the odor of cigarette smoke and chocolate.

By Sunday Robert had forgotten about the game and was driving back and forth on the freeways, half-heartedly looking for a jewelry store where he could get his Omega watch repaired. His ex-wife had given him the watch for one of their anniversaries. He arrived home at five o'clock and automatically turned the television set on. He was already sipping his second Scotch when the NFL scoreboard show announced that the Vikings had lost by ten points on two interceptions, a blocked kick, and muddled, apathetic play. The Lions might even make the playoffs. Robert stared at the television screen, reached for his wallet, and ran into the bedroom, where the bedside clock said that it was 6:15. Without coat, gloves, or hat, but warmed by the whiskey, he hurried out of the building into the park. Stumbling on the path, he at last found his way to the bench where the crank sat, tapping his feet on the ice, making metallic clicks.

"You're late," he said.

"I forgot about the game."

"Forgot?" the crank shouted. "What the hell have you been doing all day? I tried to call you!"

"I was out driving on the freeways looking for a jeweler."

"There are no jewelers on the freeways."

"I didn't consider that when I left this morning," Robert said. "I forgot about things. I didn't remember our bet until I came home and saw the wrap-up and the clips from Brent Musburger. I guess I owe you a hundred."

"That's right." Robert saw the crank's hand reaching out toward him, the palm extended.

"Well," Robert said, taking out his wallet, "I'd give you the money if I could see it."

"Give me that," the man said, grabbing the wallet. He took out several bills at random and handed it back. "This will do." He snorted. "Believe me, therapy would cost you *much* more." He rose from the bench and pushed Robert down the path. "Let's walk. I'm cold from waiting for you."

"Come in for coffee," Robert offered. He was having trouble seeing anything; it was a cloudy night with no visible moon. "Come into my apartment. It's warmer."

"No thanks. I don't get intimate."

Robert turned around and tried to see him. "Who are you? What do you do? What are you doing with me?"

The crank stood a few feet away. "I told you. My name is Oscar. I'm a lot like you: divorced, for example. I'm another victim of leisure time. I sit at a desk all day, developing projects. I used to be an alcoholic. With me it was vodka, with you it's Scotch. An old story. I have three kids, and I don't get to see them enough. In the days when boredom almost killed me I nearly put a revolver to my head. It wasn't boredom, exactly, but you understand what I mean. Now I call people up on the telephone. It's interesting. It gets me into situations. Believe me, a sane man could do much much worse. And you know what? People get the idea of what I'm doing, and they don't think I'm very strange at all. They want to talk." Robert walked under a streetlight where the path reached the sidewalk and turned around to see Oscar's face. He expected to see horrors but it was an ordinary middle-aged human face.

"Surprised?" Oscar said, and his breath blew out into the frigid air. "Everybody is getting something here. You're helping me, I'm helping you."

Robert shrugged.

"What does it take?" the crank asked. "I may have to give up on you. Listen. Tomorrow night's game on ABC is between the Bills and the Patriots. It's at Buffalo. What do you say?"

"Who cares? That's what I say."

"We'll put five hundred on it. That'll make you care."

"This is ridiculous," Robert said as they walked together

on the outer edge of the park. "First of all, I don't bet. Second, five hundred is too much. Third, who in the world cares about the Buffalo Bills and the New England Patriots?"

"If betting money on football doesn't get you interested in life," the crank asked, "what will?"

"I don't know."

"All right, make it a thousand," the crank said. "One thousand dollars. You can't spare it and I can't spare it. Now *that's* too much. I'll take the Bills. I don't give you any points. They're both erratic, mediocre teams that'll never amount to anything, unless Ron Meyer actually fixes the discipline with the Patriots, which I doubt. Is it a deal?"

"Who says you always get to decide which team you're taking? If you want Buffalo, you can have it, but I still don't have that kind of money."

"Stop being reasonable. Just do it. If you were reasonable, you wouldn't be standing out in a city park in the middle of winter with no overcoat on, talking to a stranger about football, your breath reeking of Scotch. You'd be inside a living room with your wife and kids, playing Parcheesi. Well, that's for them. This is for us. All right. Is it a deal?"

"Yes." They shook hands. "We meet out here on Tuesday night?"

"I'm sure one of us will be here," the crank said, walking away, his boots crunching in the snow.

Robert stopped at the bank during the day, and after transferring money between accounts, he drew out a thousand dollars in cash, feeling disgusted and exalted at the same time. The teller, a dark-haired woman named Robin who kept a child's sticker of a robin glued to her nameplate, stared blankly at the money as she counted it out, touching the bills tenderly with the tips of her fingers. "One hundred, two hundred, three hundred . . . ." She had painted her nails cyan. Small cameras above the windows blinked at them. Robert said, "It's for a trip," but the teller didn't stop counting, and her face showed that she didn't require an explanation. But she did say, "Enjoy it," which was new for him, at least in a bank. He put the money in his wallet and passed out of the bank's steel-perfumed air and Muzak to his car, which was still warm and started immediately.

All evening he stared at the television set, his face tight with concern. Whenever he sat down, his fat wallet pressed into his buttocks. He drank several cans of beer. His team, the Patriots, went ahead in the second quarter by two touchdowns. Joe Ferguson's passes for Buffalo throughout the first half landed on the sidelines or went high, beyond the reach of his receivers. The fans in Rich Park became great roaring animals, hating their own team in public, throwing beer cans on the field in front of network television.

But in the second half Steve Grogan couldn't move the ball for the Patriots, and the Buffalo defense held Tony Collins to the line of scrimmage. The Bills took one touchdown on a long pass from Ferguson in the third quarter, another in the fourth, and won with a field goal in the last minute from Efren Herrera.

Robert rushed out into the dark. He had remembered to wear his overcoat. He was not frightened of ice or of losing his thousand dollars in cash. He ran. "Oscar!" he shouted. His cordovan shoes sank into snow.

When he reached the park bench, there was no sign of the crank. It was a perfect Minnesota night: clear sky, stars, snow, and subzero temperatures. Robert sat down on the bench, his hands forming into fists in his coat pocket, and he shook his head against the pitch-black cold. He waited. Nobody came to take his money. The aggressive chill of the metal bench pressed hard into his thighs, and at last he stood up.

"Oscar!" he sang on two notes, like an auctioneer. "Your team came back. They won. Here I am. Come and get it." He wondered if maybe it was the beer that was making him do this. "Come and get your money."

He looked down into the bushes. "Come get your thousand dollars," he repeated. "I have it here in my wallet. I brought it in cash." In the darkness even the trees seemed interested. "Oscar!" he shouted again. "Jackpot. I have your money. You want it? It's here." He patted his wallet. Then he stopped shouting when he heard footsteps on the path somewhere in the darkness behind him. "I'm not going to wait forever," he said, loudly. "That's what I did before." It was as if he was talking to himself, and he wanted to be talking to himself if someone came up the path, a mugger, and wrapped an arm around his throat.

"Isn't anybody in this park?" he asked suddenly. He waited. "Hey you guys!" he said. "Here I am. Here I am in the place you told me to be."

But the park appeared to be empty, except for himself.

He took a long shower and settled down in front of the television set, waiting for the call that would explain everything. He was long past the news; Johnny Carson was on now. He poured himself a reasonable amount of Scotch and left the ice out of the glass.

After the first sip, which made him feel no better and no worse, just different, he tried to watch the commercials and what followed, but he kept going to the window and standing next to the Christmas tree to stare out. He turned off all the lights in the apartment except for the television set and the lights on the tree. From his front window the park seemed as cold and vacant as before. He knocked softly on the glass, opened the window, and sniffed the air for chocolate.

He walked to the bedroom, pulled two handkerchiefs out of his top dresser drawer, and blew his nose into one of them. Then, without turning on the hall lights, he walked to the kitchen, where he opened a cabinet and reached in for a box of Nabisco saltine crackers.

He took the saltines and the two handkerchiefs, the dirty one on the bottom, into the living room, where he sat down in front of the reclining chair. Opening the box of crackers, he took out two and stuffed them into his mouth. He chewed for five seconds, then said, "The quick brown fox jumped over the lazy dog." Then he sang the first two lines of the national anthem. Satisfied, he swallowed and reached in for two more crackers. Staring past the Christmas tree, he saw outside in the distance a radio transmitting tower, with its red blinking light at the top. He took the two handkerchiefs in his right hand and reached for the telephone with his left.

Taking the receiver off the hook, he covered the mouthpiece as he dialed. He had forgotten the saltines. He hung up, put two crackers in his mouth, chewed for a moment, then picked up the receiver and dialed again.

The phone rang seven times before his ex-wife answered. "Hello?" she said.

He waited, his heart pounding. Then he began. "God rest you merry, gentlemen, let nothing you dismay!" he sang, spraying cracker crumbs all over the handkerchiefs.

"Who is this?" his ex-wife said, sleepily.

"Remember Christ our Savior was born on Christmas day," he sang, stuffing more saltines into his mouth, "to save us all from Satan's power when we were gone astray. Oh, tidings of comfort—"

"—Who *is* this?" she shouted. "My God, who is this?"